THROUGH THE TEARS

Leigh M. Lorien

A NineStar Press Publication

Published by NineStar Press
P.O. Box 91792,
Albuquerque, New Mexico, 87199 USA.
www.ninestarpress.com

Through the Tears

Copyright © 2019 by Leigh M. Lorien
Cover Art by Natasha Snow Copyright © 2019
Edited by Elizabetta McKay

Printed in the USA
First Edition
July, 2019

Print ISBN: 978-1-951057-02-2

Also available in eBook, ISBN: 978-1-951057-01-5

Huge, horrid creatures with a taste for human flesh have been invading Seacliff Manor and its surrounding lands for years. Ghouls are coming from another world through portals made of magic. No one knows why or how, but nothing good ever comes with them.

During a hunting trip, Eamon encounters one such monster and falls through a portal into the ghoul's hellacious desert home world. Separated from his home, his friends, and his lover, with no magic of his own and no sign of other life, Eamon expects to die there...until an encounter with a lone stranger gives him hope. There is a way home. But can Eamon survive alone in ghoul-infested terrain long enough to get there?

Worlds away, the Lord of Seacliff Manor is determined to bring Eamon home. Despite all evidence to the contrary, Rafe knows his human lover is alive. It's just a matter of finding out where. To that end, Rafe has a plan. It's dangerous, perhaps even suicidal, but he'll do anything to save the man he loves.

From different sides of the galaxy, the lovers fight monsters and seek magic with one goal in mind: reunion. Monsters aren't the only things they'll have to defeat to find their way back to each other, and the horrors uncovered along the way may be more than they can handle.

Chapter One

RAFE

The body lay at the base of a maple tree in a crumpled heap of leathery gray flesh and black blood. Rafe studied it for a long time. Its fanged mouth hung open, eyes like black marbles gazing lifelessly at him, hands with hawk-like talons curled into loose fists in the grass. It was more than capable of killing a human—gods, it was probably capable of killing *him*. He turned away, forcing down the momentary surge of fear as he took in the scene, playing through the information he had.

Eamon, Lionel, Rose, and Tuomas had been hunting that morning, as Eamon had said they planned to do. Lionel was training a new bird. They were well armed. No one left the stronghold unarmed these days. Ghoul incursions were growing more frequent, and the filthy things were getting bolder by the day. Rafe had wanted to send an escort with them but let his lover talk him out of it. *We'll be fine. We're barely going past the village.*

But they weren't fine. Lionel's bird didn't return when it should have. The ghoul had crept up on them while they were distracted.

Signs of the struggle were obvious all around the body. Broken twigs, displaced leaves, mud spatters up the trunks of the trees. The humans had come out victorious. Three of them had, anyway.

Thirty or so feet beyond the ghoul's body, a cliff dropped into the sea. Ignoring his audience—the three humans who'd returned, as well as two of his rin retainers—Rafe walked past the ghoul's corpse, inspecting the grass between the site of the attack and the edge of the cliff. Clods of soil lay in heaps where massive claws had raked it up. He wished there was some indication of Eamon's movements, but the ghoul's weight and erratic assault covered all sign of his human lover. Blood spatters painted the grass black. Rafe didn't need to touch or taste the drying liquid to know it was not human. Not Eamon's. The rotten stench of ghoul blood was as foul as raw sewage and, for once, he envied the humans their inferior senses. Someone had hurt it, and badly, right here. Eamon was not a close-quarters fighter. He was barely a fighter at all. If Rafe were a gambler, he'd put his money on Lionel and the longsword he wore.

"You say he fell," Rafe stated. It wasn't a question. Rose had spoken for the group, told their story in a quavering voice. If the two men were hoping Rafe would show mercy to a teary-eyed woman and thus to them as well, they were all mistaken.

"Yes, Lord," Rose said. "Th-the ghoul tackled him, and they rolled, and...I'm not certain, I mean I-I didn't see it myself, Lord, but...Eamon was gone when..."

Rafe walked to the very edge of the cliff and leaned forward to look down, grateful for an excuse to breathe air untainted by blood. The tension level behind him rose tangibly, but no one rushed forward to drag him back. He was their lord, not a child to be scolded for putting himself in danger. Hundreds of feet below, waves crashed and roared over a beach of jagged stone. Even with his sensitive rin hearing, little more than the faintest whisper reached Rafe's ears from this distance. There was no question that a fall from this height meant no survival for a human. No matter what awaited at the end of the fall, no matter how strong the human.

And yet...

He had not felt Eamon die. Rafe had never had a bound companion die, so, he didn't know from experience what it would feel like, but he'd heard others speak of it. He'd expected something...worse. He should have experienced fear as Eamon fell, pain as he crashed to the ground and his body shattered against the rocks below. It would have dropped him to his knees, put him in a state of shock.

Instead, there was a sharp surprise, fear, and then...an absence. Eamon simply was not there. He wasn't alive, but neither was he dead.

"You are aware Eamon is bound to me?" Rafe turned to the humans, and they all bowed their heads, nodding and avoiding his eyes. "You should have *protected him.*"

The wind off the sea howled and whipped his dark hair around his head. Everything was cast in a dusky gray—the winter sun had not shown its face for days, and the choppy sea below was the color of cold steel. Standing at least a head taller than the tallest of the three humans, Rafe was no stranger to intimidation tactics. It wasn't his preferred modus operandi—physical threats were so pedestrian—but it was easy, and with the gaping absence of Eamon distracting him, it was all he managed.

"I'm sure they did their best, my lord," Kiran, his retainer, said softly.

Rafe continued to aim a cold gaze at the humans.

"I'm sure. Have search parties organized. Comb the beach and the forest in this area. I did not feel him die."

And if he was mistaken and Eamon *was* dead…The words hurt as they formed in his mind, but he forced them out. "If you find him, or his body, bring him home."

Kiran bowed his head and rushed toward the manor to find willing and able individuals to carry out the command. Wind continued to buffet Rafe's side and face, tangling his hair as it whipped around. In his imagination, Eamon was scolding him as he worked a brush through Rafe's hair as he did every night. *Would it kill you to tie your hair back once in a while? It's like you tangle it on purpose.*

If it weren't tangled, I wouldn't need you to brush it, would I? Rafe would reply and grin in the mirror at his lover. The thought of the familiar teasing almost made him smile. Almost.

"M-my lord," Tuomas ventured, stepping forward as Rafe returned to the ghoul's body. "We would like to join the search parties, if we may."

Rafe shook his head. "No. Take this body to the manor. Have it burned."

The three humans exchanged wide-eyed glances. The ghoul was larger than all three of them combined. Heavy as it was, it would take them hours to drag it to the manor. It seemed a mild punishment in Rafe's eyes, for letting his lover fall over a cliff.

Tuomas and Lionel were unbound and had been for as long as Rafe had known them. Rose was bound to Elena, the manor's doctor, and lived in the manor with her, while the two human men lived in the village outside the manor walls—together, if Rafe was not mistaken. Eamon had lived with Tuomas for some time, until he came to Rafe's attention, and still spent the night in Tuomas's village home on occasion. Perhaps it was cruel to punish the three of them in any way for what had happened. They were likely hurting as much as Rafe, but they were not bound to Eamon. They could not feel his absence, like the loss of a limb or an eye or an ear, like a crushing emptiness where, until mere hours ago, there had been a warm, bright presence every day for the past ten years.

"Stay with them," Rafe instructed his second retainer, Orienna. "See that we lose no one else to rogue ghouls today."

The woman bowed. "What of you, my lord?"

"I'm in a mood to rip something's throat out," he said coldly. "Let the filth try."

Chapter Two

EAMON

After a brief drop, Eamon's body impacted stone, and all the air left his lungs in a startled grunt. He rolled gracelessly down a slope, every inch of his body hitting stone along the way, before coming to a stop in a tangled heap at the bottom. A groan eked out, and when he'd caught his breath, when the world was no longer spinning and black at the edges, he dragged himself to his knees and looked around.

One minute, he'd been wrestling with something intent on eating him, and the next minute, he found himself here. Rafe's manor had been built near the sea, and Eamon had lived in the area for most of his adult life. He was accustomed to salty air, thick grass, and a near-constant breeze.

This place could not be more different.

Eamon knelt in a pile of scree at the base of a rocky hill. When he twisted around, he saw nothing but stones and sand. Grayish-red rock stretched out to oblivion, all the way to where it met the orange sky at the horizon. A handful of dead-looking plants spotted the landscape, and above him, two white-hot suns shone. *Two suns in an orange sky.*

Two suns...

"Oh gods." The words came out in a whimper as realization dawned. His heart rate picked up and sweat broke out across his skin. Twisting in place again, he searched in vain for a familiar landmark, for anything to point the way to home, anything to convince him this was not real or that everything would be okay. His gaze turned back up to the hill he'd fallen down, searching for the portal which must have formed to let him through, but it was gone.

This was the ghoul's world. Two suns flying in an orange sky, days like fire, nights like ice, ground of stone and air of sand—Rafe had always teased him for reading so many history books. *No one travels like that anymore,* he'd said when he caught Eamon in the library with a tome about the open times. *No one but the king and his chosen few.* And lately, unwelcome ghouls.

But the worlds still exist, Eamon had returned, picking his feet up off the chair across from him so his lover could join him. *Don't you find it interesting? I wish such travel were still common. I would like to go to another world, just to say I'd done it.*

This was not the one he would have chosen. This was where the ghouls came from. Those monstrosities had been showing up near Seacliff. Creatures with no respect for life, no understanding of human language. Beasts no better than the wild animals in the forest. Eaters of human flesh.

"Gods!" he said, his voice shamefully high-pitched. A sob caught in his chest, and he had to fight to breathe, dragging in gasps of parched air. Where was the ghoul that had brought him here?

Eamon got to his feet, stumbling on the uneven stony ground. His head spun as he rose, toppling him back to his knees, but he didn't stay down. He sucked in quick, shallow breaths and forced himself up again, cringing as the world darkened and a blade drove through his skull. He turned around in a full circle one way and then the other, but the stony expanse stretched far beyond him in every direction. The ghoul wasn't nearby. Perhaps it had thrown him through and gone after the others. It might return through any minute to...to eat him. He patted himself down frantically, checking to be certain his bow had not broken in the struggle or fall, grasping the arrows in the quiver at his hip. Only five. He'd had at least a dozen this morning! *Shit*! Panic drove him through the scree, gasping in the dry air, losing precious moisture through sweat and tears.

He couldn't feel Rafe. Ever since they'd undergone the ritual of bondage, which entwined their lives and linked their every thought and emotion, Rafe had been a constant presence in his mind. But now, in another world, only silence shared his mind, and the realization brought him to his knees again, shaking and nauseous. He was alone.

Alone.

If he tried hard enough, he might trick himself into hearing his lover's voice in his mind, familiar from a hundred memories of breakdowns like this.

You're panicking, love. Rafe was always patient and calm in the face of Eamon's baseless terror. *I'm here for you, Eamon.* Despite all his better-than-human senses and abilities, Rafe was unable to vanquish this monster. He'd expressed frustration to Eamon more than once about his impotence in the face of Eamon's fear, and Eamon hated to put his lover through such pain. Even so, Rafe was always there, physically or mentally, if Eamon needed him.

Now, he was not.

It took a long time for Eamon's body and mind to settle enough for rational thought. The ghoul hadn't yet returned through the portal to finish him, which meant—he hoped—it was dead. Tuomas and Lionel and Rose must have killed it.

Even so, it didn't mean much for him. The ability to form rifts between worlds was rare. No one in Rafe's household or village was able to do it, which meant no rescue. He was trapped.

The suns were setting by the time Eamon had collected himself. He sipped from his waterskin, just enough to moisten his throat. He'd refilled it just after midday, so he had enough for a day if he was careful.

In this place, though, enough for a day or so might as well have been nothing.

In the distance, mountains stretched up into the orange sky. It was impossible to judge how far he stood from them, but they were the best hope he had. As the suns fell and the air cooled, Eamon got up and began to walk.

Chapter Three

EAMON

The landscape was, for the most part, level. Gentle slopes rose here and there, and occasionally, a rocky crag jutted up from the reddish foundation, but as Eamon walked all night, shivering in the starlit darkness, he found it an endless monotony of gravel and stone. A few times, a scraggly plant interrupted the rock, and he licked the dew off the narrow leaves to stretch his water supply, but he didn't encounter a single animal. In a way, it was a blessing. At least he didn't encounter a ghoul.

As day approached, he found an outcropping to press himself into, hoping for shade. The thought of sleeping in a world where humans were considered a delicacy was ludicrous. He'd been in this realm for over twelve hours, he guessed, and hadn't seen a sign of life beyond plants, but that didn't mean a ghoul couldn't pop out of the ether and land on his head the moment he dozed off. Why any creature, ghoul or not, would choose this wasteland as an arrival point, Eamon had no idea, but if one had done it, others might have reasons as well. Ghouls were hardier than delicate little humans, and travel between worlds was not well understood. There had been a time when it was commonplace—trade routes had existed between worlds dominated by ghouls and rin and humans and all sorts of others—but when humans tired of being on the menu, a sect of travelers sealed off the worlds, leaving many behind and taking the secrets of world travel with them.

Stripping off his cloak in an attempt to stay cool once the hot suns had risen, Eamon crammed himself back into the nook under his chosen crag and closed his eyes. If nothing else, his eyes would benefit from a rest from the ceaseless casting about for life, danger, help, food, or water he'd been doing all night.

As he lay on his side, the hard, uneven ground and sharp stones dug into his hip and arm. He shifted to push those away and only succeeded in moving onto others. The rock smelled like heat and dust, his cracked lips were sore, his throat burned, and worst of all, his stomach writhed in hunger. He had a bit of food, but after walking all night and getting no closer to the illusory mountains, Eamon thought it best to ration it carefully.

Exhaustion caught up to him before long, and he slept.

"My lord!"

Kiran, Rafe's most loyal retainer, threw open the door to the library. Eamon jerked awake at the sound and grumbled, but at a touch from Rafe, didn't bother to sit up. A nap with his head pillowed on his lover's thigh was not the most compromising position Kiran had ever caught them in.

"What is it, Kiran?" Rafe asked, his hand caressing Eamon's cheek as he rolled over to face their visitor. Eamon had always liked the rin and didn't mind his visit.

Kiran was panting, shoulders heaving and dark skin flushed as if he'd just run all the way from the village, or even beyond.

"A-a ghoul, my lord."

Rafe's body and mind tensed. The sharp edge echoed into his own consciousness, and Eamon sat up, fully awake now. Rafe let him rise, lifting the caressing hand off Eamon's face.

"Explain."

When Kiran had enough breath, he said, "I was in the village, my lord. Feeding. Dina wanted to walk, so we walked, and...I saw it with my own eyes, my lord, at the edge of the cliff, climbing up over it. I came straight here to—"

It was a good thing Eamon had sat up because Rafe leaped to his feet and tossed aside the book he'd been reading. "It's there now? Within walking distance of the village?"

Kiran's gold eyes widened in horror when he realized his error.

"Show me," Rafe demanded, taking hold of his retainer's face in both hands.

Their eyes met, and Eamon knew his lover was seeing Kiran's memories. Kiran swayed, his mind out of his control, but maintained his footing.

When he'd gotten what he needed, Rafe planted a quick kiss on Kiran's forehead. Eamon was already getting to his feet to help support the other rin in the dizzying wake of having his mind read. Rafe left them with barely a word.

"Are you all right?" Eamon asked. Kiran nodded, pulling out of his hands to follow their lord. Eamon reached out along the bond he shared with Rafe and spoke into his lover's mind as he followed Kiran out of the library.

I'm coming with you.

No.

Yes.

Rafe strode down the hall toward Eamon and Kiran, and Eamon stopped and drew himself up to his full height—still shorter than Rafe and Kiran, but somewhat imposing among his own kind. Rafe ignored Kiran and looped an arm around Eamon, pulling him aside to speak in soft tones.

"Don't be foolish. You don't have to prove yourself to anyone."

"Is it foolish to want to be at my lover's side when he faces danger?"

"These things eat humans, Eamon."

"I know. I'm sure they don't hesitate to kill rin either."

A muscle clenched in Rafe's jaw, and for a split second, Eamon feared a more vehement argument was about to break out, but, instead, Rafe cupped his face in both hands and kissed him hard on the mouth. It was a brief, passionate touch, then Rafe pulled away and their eyes met.

"I love you for your bravery and your foolishness in equal measures, Eamon." He gave his brave, foolish human lover a rare smile, whispered, "Be careful," and continued the way he'd been headed, toward the armory. Eamon took a deep breath and let it out to calm his racing pulse, then followed.

A short time later, armored and armed, Rafe, Kiran, Eamon, and six others rode out from the manor. Rafe's lands weren't vast, but he took his duty as lord and protector seriously. The manor house sat above the village on the cleared slope leading up to the cliff, and a wide dirt road led from its gates, down through the village and beyond, into the forest.

"Lead the way, Kiran," Rafe said, pulling up the reins to let his retainer take charge of the small retinue. The rin moved his dun mare to the front, and Rafe fell in at his flank, Eamon just behind them. Rafe's tension and fury dogged at Eamon and tightened his chest with sympathetic anger. A ghoul daring to come this close to Rafe's lands was an affront to him, and daring to enter this world at all was an affront to all rin. The creatures had to know the danger they faced if they dared cross into this world. The filth was getting bolder.

The village was in an uproar, but cheers broke out when Rafe's company came into sight. Kiran no longer needed to lead, as the villagers—rin and humans alike—began pointing toward the edge of the forest, shouting and crying.

"It took Winston!" a woman shrieked, sobbing. Rafe dismounted, and the crowd parted to allow him through. He went to her and took her hands.

"Your husband?"

"N-no," she gasped. "My son. My husband went after it."

The lord's anger surged up into a white-hot rage. Eamon swallowed, his hands clutching the reins so tightly it hurt. Though the anger was not directed at him—it never was—the power of it overwhelmed him. Rafe turned to the crowd.

"Has anyone else gone after it?"

"My son," an old man said. "And his wife."

"Anyone else?" Rafe demanded when no one else spoke up. After a brief silence, he returned to his mount. "No one else goes after it. We will handle it. If your loved ones are alive, we will bring them back."

Rafe urged his gray stallion into a canter, and the others followed suit. It only took moments to find the villagers, and with them, their quarry. They were fighting it, and from the sound of things, losing. A body lay not far from the fight, chunks of flesh stripped away from bone, belly torn open so deep the spine was visible inside. Eamon turned his gaze away quickly, wondering if it was Winston, his father, or the old man's son.

The ghoul towered over its human opponents—its prey. Twice their height, it was vaguely humanoid, with longer arms, a hunched back, and a dog-like snout. Its body lacked hair and the blood-spattered skin looked coarse and dry like a reptile. Eamon drew a deep breath to calm the immediate fear, and the rancid, coppery stench of fresh death assaulted his nose. Humans smelled the same in death as any other animal. He shook himself. Those were not the kinds of thoughts he needed to be having right now.

Rafe's cold, tightly focused anger surged over Eamon like a tidal wave, drowning out the panic. It was a trade Eamon was glad to make. He let Rafe's icy fury focus him.

"Eamon," Rafe said in a calm, sharp voice, "draw its attention, please."

Without question, Eamon slid an arrow from the quiver at his hip, lifted his bow off his back, and took quick but careful aim. The weapon and movements were so familiar from hundreds of hunts it didn't shake his calm to know he was aiming at something horrible and foreign. He released. The ghoul moved at the last second, sparing it the loss of an eye, but gaining it a charming lip piercing. It let out a deep, guttural roar and turned *toward them. Rafe, Kiran, and the other rin moved in front of Eamon to protect him, but he did not protest. He was an archer, not a swordsman. He would leave the flesh-rending and gut-stabbing to his lover.*

Chapter Four

EAMON

When Eamon woke, the first shift of his body sent pain pulsing through every inch of him. Falling through the portal and rolling down a hill had given him a solid foundation of bruises and cuts. Walking all night meant the muscles of his legs and feet were stiff and sore.

Worst of all, his bare arms and face were in utter agony. He groaned as he opened his eyes and tried to sit up. Even the smallest movement twisted and pulled at the hot, tight skin, and he stared at his arms for several minutes. His skin, usually pale, had turned vibrant red everywhere it was not covered by clothing. It looked like he'd walked through fire. It *felt* like he'd walked through fire, hot and tender to touch. What had happened while he was sleeping?

Something seemed to crush his chest and breathing became difficult. Panic, all too familiar, washed over him. Was this as bad as a burn? He needed Elena, the manor's physician. He needed Rafe. Again, in desperation, he tried to reach out along their bond. Since the moment they said the words and sealed it in blood, an invisible tether had formed between their minds. At first, it had been overwhelming to have two sets of feedback, two awarenesses. They'd quickly found fun ways to use it, but had to seek out help from one of Rafe's more experienced advisors to learn to dull it, push it to the back of their mind, and, occasionally, seal themselves off from it altogether. Now, though, Eamon craved the overwhelming knowledge of Rafe. He hunted in his mind for the slightest inkling of hunger that was not his, a restful feeling to indicate sleep, pleasure, yearning, *something*, a spark of an emotion, *anything*! He focused into the emptiness and waited in silence for something in return, but nothing came.

A sudden image filled his mind—Rafe lying broken and bleeding on the deep green grass, ribs visible through the gaping bloody hole where the ghoul had torn his clothes and flesh away with one horrible bite, dead eyes staring up into the twilight without seeing its muted pinks and purples. Eamon gasped a breath of air like sand across the open cracks on his lips, the raw soreness of his throat. Rafe could be *dead*.

There had been other ghouls, after the one that had killed Winston's father, but Eamon had always been there with Rafe, had his back, saw what they were up against. Being trapped in this awful desert was bad. He might die here, which was horrifying. But Rafe might die, and Eamon would never know, never get to say goodbye—the thought was too much to bear. Eamon curled in on himself, wheezing. When his left hand grasped his right bicep in a self-comforting hug, he bit back a scream. The pain of the touch on his burnt skin jolted thoughts into his mind. *Don't cry. You're in a desert. You can't afford to waste those tears.* It was easier thought than done, though, and he wasted a shameful amount of water before getting himself under control.

With shaking hands, he found his waterskin and carefully took a mouthful, pushing it around with his tongue to moisten every nook and cranny of his gums and cheeks, swallowing in measures to make it last as long as possible.

The heinous suns were setting now, splashing red and pink across the cloudless sky. He was still alone in this stone-riddled wasteland. *Since the alternative is probably to be eaten alive, I'll take the crushing loneliness.* Eamon carefully pulled his cloak around himself, cringing when it brushed across his injured skin, and got up. The mountains seemed closer now. It had been hard to tell how much progress he'd made in the darkness last night, but he guessed it would take another night or two before he reached the foothills.

What he expected to find there, he didn't know. Water? Water would be good. Food? Yes, food was vital.

People?

Eamon wasn't sure humans even lived in this world. Long ago, all sentient species had intermingled on all the worlds—the "open times," as they were now called—but after the seclusion, he didn't know. No one did. With the way ghouls had been coming through dimensions and invading rin lands to prey on their humans, he figured humans must be pretty scarce here. Recently, there'd been accounts of ghouls taking humans from villages in his world and disappearing back through the tears into their own world, but if those people were in the grip of a ghoul, they were as good as dead.

So, no, maybe not people.

Maybe...nothing. Maybe he'd find water and food, but...no people. And he'd spend the rest of his life hiding, alone, hoping not to die at the hands—or teeth—of a hellacious monster. If this were the case, "the rest of his life" wouldn't be very long. He would rather take his own life than spend sixty years shuddering in the mountains of this horrid wasteland.

Don't think like that. You'll find a way. Rafe will find a way. For now, stay alive.

And so he walked, pausing only to nibble his rations and sip water. His arms and face ached, but he kept his cloak on and hood up. The suns had set, but the cloak protected his injuries from the lingering heat of the air.

By nightfall, his nervous glances, his searches of the horizon for massive monsters, dwindled to nothing. He had enough energy to watch his feet, to avoid tripping over large stones and to kneel and suck dew off the leaves of occasional plants, but as the night wore on, it became more difficult to get up once he'd knelt, and he worried he wouldn't have the energy to rise next time. Cold sank into his flesh and down to his bones. At first, he had the presence of mind to flex his hands, keep the blood flowing to warm his bare fingers, but as his exhaustion deepened, he let the numbness take over.

When the first pink tint was visible on the horizon, Eamon looked up toward the mountains. The craggy peaks rose high in his sight, and though he saw no signs of life on them, he did see shade. Shelter.

Half a day. It couldn't take more to get there, surely. And then he'd be able to rest.

He paused for water, a bit more food—he had enough for another day at the rate he was going, but best not to think about it right now—and then he kept walking.

HIS LEGS GAVE out for the first time not long after both suns had crested the horizon. He got back up, but not long after, his toe caught on a rock and he went down again, this time grinding his shin against the stone. His leather boots protected him from bloodying himself, but the impact would surely leave another bruise.

And yet he got up. Kept moving.

Rafe's face swam in his mind, his long black hair, soft brown skin, vibrant blue eyes. He always looked so intense. Even when he'd just woken up, his gaze cut straight through Eamon's chest and into his heart. His smiles were rare and fleeting, and Eamon treasured every glimpse of one. Rafe favored him with smiles more often as time went on. Eamon liked to think he was softening up his lord and lover, giving Rafe a reason and outlet to express happiness.

Humans were necessary for rin survival, but that didn't mean they always bound with a human, nor did it mean every human allowed them to feed from them. Those who did bond didn't always do it out of love or intimacy. Bound humans gained some impressive benefits from their rin companions, and some bindings were simply business transactions. Rafe and Eamon had a special relationship, a camaraderie and companionship beyond necessity or mutual benefit and into the realm of emotions. Rafe had never been romantically involved with anyone before. It had taken a long time to get him to open up. Eamon would be damned if after years of earning Rafe's love and trust he'd just turn over and die at the first major obstacle.

Staggering across the final stretch to the foot of the mountains became an exercise in willpower alone. He fell countless times, scraping his palms and knees on stone and scree, embedding tiny shards of rock in his flesh. Everything hurt...or at least, everything *should* have hurt, but Eamon was somewhere beyond noticing it. His vision swam, his head throbbed, and bile stung the back of his throat as he fought against nausea.

He didn't realize when he'd reached the base of the mountains. His feet carried him up a slope, and the change in incline tripped him flat on his face. This time, he didn't bother to get up. He should have been sweating more than he was. In fact, he was *cold*. When he tried to strip off his cloak to absorb some of the warm sun, his hands were shaking so badly it was impossible to undo the clasp at his throat.

"Gods *dammit!*" he shouted, but the noise came out as little more than a croak. Too much sun. Too much...

SOMETHING STRANGE WOKE Eamon. Something... wet. He jerked in surprise.

Rain.

Rain?

Rain!

Still nauseous from exhaustion, but not quite as dizzy, he rolled onto his back and opened his mouth. A steady, pleasantly warm rainfall, unlike the cold sleet he was used to at home, moistened his cracked lips and tongue in a matter of seconds. Eamon might have cried in joy. *Rain.*

A rivulet poured down the slope beside him. He rolled again, pressing his face into it, heedless of the dirt and mud, and drank. It was hot from running across the baked stone, but it was water, and it showed no signs of stopping. He dragged his empty waterskin off his belt and filled it from the newborn stream, close to crying with relief at the sensation of moisture spilling across his fingers.

Reinvigorated, he ate half of his remaining food and then looked up the slope, trying to work out a plan of action. The path he was on, if it could be called a path, climbed up and curved out of sight. These mountains, at least this low in the range, seemed to be easy to traverse. There were no sheer stone walls in sight. If he found food, he might actually have a chance!

A sound reached him from...somewhere. Still sitting on the ground, enjoying the rain, Eamon didn't give it his attention at first, but then there it was again. He recognized it this time. The sound of a fight. Steel impacting...something. He scrambled to his feet, waited for the rush of dizziness to pass, lifted his bow, and nocked an arrow before creeping up the hill toward the sound.

Around the bend and some distance up, a small, cloaked figure with a sword was facing off against a ghoul. Alone. A human?! Eamon's heart sped up, and he pressed himself against the stone, searching his mind for the calm of a hunt. It refused to come to him. Between his swimming head, racing heart, and the roiling sea of his belly, calm was not an option.

Someone screamed, high and startled, and Eamon peeked around the stone to see the monster had its human opponent pinned to the ground with one huge clawed foot.

Deep breaths. Eamon lifted the bow and a whimper left him as the necessary motion with his right arm pulled burnt skin taut and twisted. His eyes watered, and he tried to calm down, but the ghoul was at least twice the size of a human. Even if he missed its vitals, he might draw its attention. He loosed and watched the arrow embed deep in the thing's shoulder. It roared and its attention shifted from its pinned target to him. When it lifted its foot to come after him, the cloaked person rolled and regained their sword quickly enough to slash at the creature's hind leg. It staggered. Eamon groaned as he moved his arm for another arrow and, again, contorted his injured skin. The ghoul seemed conflicted about who to pursue, but after a second, spun and returned to its original target. Eamon leaned a shoulder against the stone, dizzy and nauseous again. Shit! He didn't have time for this!

The human circled around, putting their back to Eamon, but giving him an opening to shoot the thing in the face again. He took advantage of the maneuver and, through pain and blurred vision, loosed another arrow. It didn't go into the ghoul's face as he intended. Instead, it went low and—did the arrow hit the human as it zipped past, or did it just appear to?

The person glanced at him, bellowed something he didn't catch, and returned their attention to the battle just in time to dodge a swing of the ghoul's claws. The stranger staggered and the thing got the upper hand again. It had the human on the run, though they were quick and able to dodge the attacks of their larger, slower opponent. With a deep breath, Eamon staggered forward to decrease the distance between himself and his target.

Ghouls were as varied in size, shape, and color as humans and rin. In fact, comparing ghouls and humans wasn't fair. They were closer to animals than humans—as there were many kinds of dogs with vastly different appearances, behaviors, and purposes, so it was with ghouls. Some were large and dry-skinned. Some had fur, some had feathers. They were small, barely larger than a human, or so large they could swallow a human whole, if the books in Rafe's library were accurate. This one appeared amphibious, frog-like, its huge gray-green head and mouth so wide he feared it would whip out a long, sticky tongue and suck him or the other person in with one bite.

As the human continued to dodge and slash at the ghoul, Eamon nocked an arrow, pulled, and loosed it at the thing's big head. This time, his aim was true. The arrow drove into the ghoul's eye, bursting the viscous orb in a splash of blood. It roared, and he nocked and loosed again, this time piercing its throat. Blood gushed down its body. It thrashed, clawed at its own face and neck, slammed itself against the rock...and fell, twitching. A long tongue lolled out of its mouth. Eamon sank to his knees, then doubled over and threw up all the murky water he'd gleefully swallowed moments before.

The stranger addressed him, their voice low and angry, and Eamon turned his gaze toward them. A scarf was wrapped around their head under the cloak's hood, so only dark, narrowed eyes were visible. They didn't move any closer, and Eamon wasn't sure he'd be able to get up just yet, so they stayed at a distance from each other, squinting through the rain.

"My name is Eamon. I'm sorry if I hurt you." He forced a grimace of a smile. "I'm...not feeling well." Hopefully, killing the ghoul would earn him some credit, and this other person wouldn't leave him to die for accidentally shooting them in the leg—if he had.

The other person glanced over their shoulder at the dead ghoul and then closed the distance to where Eamon knelt. It was difficult to tell anything about them under the ragged clothes and cloak. They were small in stature and build, but their size didn't mean anything. As he'd just seen, they were more than able to handle themself.

They spoke again when they were closer, and the language was familiar. Without the edge of anger or fear, the voice was soft and high. It wasn't Eamon's native language—why would he expect someone from another world to speak the same language?—but he recognized it, at least in part. It sounded like Caddenese, a human language that had fallen out of common use hundreds of years ago when humans and rin began bonding. In human-only communities, it was sometimes still the dominant tongue, but Eamon hadn't lived in a human-only community since his childhood.

He tried to piece together a sentence, to explain what he was doing, what he needed, so this stranger could understand him, but in his bleary state, all he recalled was a rite he'd had drilled into his head by his family's worship leader. He muttered it under his breath, playing through the words until he got to the phrase he wanted.

The stranger spoke, sharply, and this time, Eamon picked out a few words: "What, you, here?" It wasn't hard to guess what they meant.

He tried to answer with his remembered phrases. They meant something like: "Though I may stray, a place remains for me at home, always. Though I may be lost, the way can be found if only I ask for guidance." It was meant as a reminder the gods would watch over them. But here in this world, this stranger was the only one Eamon expected to give him any guidance.

Eamon gazed up at them from his kneeling position and blinked as rain got in his eyes. They were staring at him with suspicion. He turned his focus to the ground and their boots, not unlike his—thick, stiff leather encasing their legs all the way to the knee.

A long pause, then the stranger bent and grabbed Eamon's arm, pulling. Getting the hint, he struggled to his feet and gratefully accepted the support. It was impossible to guess where they were going, but in his situation, he'd rather go *anywhere* with another person than stay where he was, alone.

Chapter Five

BEAH

The archer was heavy and clumsy with weakness. Beah took most of his weight as they made their way to the cave where he'd been staying for...gods, about a full cycle now. By the time they reached it, it seemed all the stranger could do was flop limply onto the ground and whisper a breathy, broken thanks. His quote from the Rite of Devotion had Beah intrigued, especially since he didn't seem to speak Caddenese as his main language. His clothes were strange and not at all suited to a desert, his skin so pale he never should have stepped out in the sun without every inch of his body covered.

Orange sunlight filtered through the narrow cave entrance, splashing an unruly shape across the far wall. Beah wanted to get a fire going for light—the temperature in the cave stayed much lower than the sunbaked desert outside, so the heat would be welcome before long—but fire was the last thing this stranger needed. Making do with the sunlight, Beah knelt by his motionless visitor, inspecting his sun-reddened face and arms, pinching a spot of unburnt skin to check how hydrated he was. The stranger lay through it placidly, breathing hard. He was sun-poisoned, dehydrated, and heatsick. Lucky to be alive. What was this pale foreigner doing in the desert?

"What is your name?" Beah asked. The man's brows furrowed in confusion, and Beah sighed. He patted his chest. "Beah." It was the first time he'd introduced himself by his chosen name, first time he'd given this name to someone who hadn't known him by his other name. Something tense in his mind seemed to release, and he repeated himself with more confidence. "I'm Beah." He patted the stranger's chest and lifted his eyebrows in question. The response came in a whispery breath over parched lips.

"Eamon."

"Eamon," Beah repeated, and the man nodded. Good.

Beah grabbed his waterskin and helped Eamon drink. He had a thousand questions for the archer, but they would wait. He'd treated dozens of cases of sun-poisoning—usually in foolish children and the elderly who overestimated themselves—and he knew the danger Eamon was in if he didn't cool down and rehydrate soon. Eamon, though, seemed unable to let his curiosity wait. His brows furrowed between swallows of water, and he finally spoke in halting Caddenese.

"I did not know...there are human...from this place." Then, after a second of intense scrutiny of Beah's face, he said, "Human?"

"Yes," Beah said, but hesitated to reveal his face to this stranger just yet. Even as sick as he was, once Eamon saw Beah's hairless face and smooth throat, there'd be no way he'd take him for anything but a girl. He might disguise his body under loose robes, but nothing would convince this stranger once he saw his face. "I'm human." Then, riding on the buzz of adrenaline: "I'm a man, like you."

He pressed the waterskin to Eamon's lips again to quiet him, ignoring the sudden shakiness in his hands at the admission. Eamon didn't question it; he just drank. It was a strange question, come to think of it. What else did Eamon think Beah could be, besides human? Beah dismissed his curiosity to care for his patient. "You must undress."

Eamon looked confused, and Beah reached out to unclasp the hook holding his cloak around his neck. The stranger let out a startled noise and tried to slap Beah's hand away, but in his weakened state, he merely pawed at it like a kitten.

"You are too hot," Beah said, trying to speak slowly for the sickly stranger's benefit even as he continued trying to undress him. The foreign clothes were odd, with a dozen buckles and clasps around waist and chest. No wonder he was overheating, wearing this awful leather garb. Though, at least he'd had the sense not to take it off and expose his entire torso to the sun.

Eamon was protesting, trying to get away, but all he succeeded in doing was working himself up so much he threw up the water he'd just drank. Beah took advantage of his distracted heaves and gags to unclasp all the buckles within reach, including Eamon's belt and boots. When the man limply flopped onto his back, shivering, Beah began peeling him out of his clothes. As he did, he admired the way the thick leather was shaped, giving a contoured appearance to the body beneath it. Perhaps if Beah wore clothing like this, it would help compress and constrain parts of his body he did not like to see...

Once the stranger was down to his breeches, Beah sprinkled water over him. The rain had to have helped— the rain might have been the only reason he wasn't baked alive on a slab of stone somewhere—but he needed to cool down a lot more. He was speaking, babbling in his native language. From the way his head lolled and his unfocused eyes stared, it was safe to assume none of his words would have made sense even if he'd been speaking a language Beah understood.

"What are you doing out here, Eamon?" Beah muttered, helping his delirious visitor drink a bit of water.

He ducked out of the cave once to refill his and the stranger's waterskins from a nearby pool of rainwater, and when he returned, the man was asleep, chest heaving, his skin prickled all over. The sunburn to his arms and face was serious, and without having to worry about Eamon fighting him, Beah took the time to apply a sticky green salve to the injured skin. A careful measure of snake venom mixed with the salve allowed it to numb the painful area, and the sticky substance, milked from the leaves of a shade-dwelling succulent cactus, had healing properties especially good for burns of this sort.

He sat vigil by Eamon's side, working to cool him with splashes of precious water, ignoring the voice in his head screaming *wasteful!* The rain would deepen the pool Beah had been drawing water from, but even if it dried up, a day and a half's walk would get him to the river. He didn't disparage about water "wasted" to help save this man's life.

He did disparage about the creature lying dead in the sun only a brief distance from the cave where they now rested. It had come close to killing him. He should have let it—all must die here, after all. His mother would drop of heart failure on the spot if she knew he'd attacked it and allowed it to be killed. Killing a morroul was a crime punishable by execution. They were the god's hands in this realm. Two cycles ago, before he saw what he'd seen, such consequences might have worried him more than they did now. Two cycles ago, when he was still in his village, living in his mother's home, he may have worried about execution.

Now, he worried more about the meat going bad in the sun before he could harvest it. Morroul were not godly creatures. If they were godly creatures, the priestess would not have been able to get rid of them. If they were godly, a couple arrows from a dying man would not have killed them. They were animals, just like the lizards and beetles he'd been eating for days, and he was starving.

A morroul of such size would feed him for a long time, if he got the meat cleaned, stripped, and dried before it spoiled. But to do so he would have to leave Eamon's side, which didn't sit well with him.

Beah stared at Eamon as he slept. This was the first human he'd seen since leaving the village. He was tall and pale, which marked him as a foreigner without question. The people in these parts were brown-skinned and not so large, though Beah was short even by his people's standards. It was a curse in many ways. It amazed him that Eamon had made it through the desert alive. He had no supplies. The pack he'd had on his back was flat and empty, though perhaps he'd run out only days ago and had made it this far on willpower alone. Impressive. Still, he'd never seen a person so pale. Where had he come from? What was this man doing so far from home? How had he *survived* this long?

The bow Eamon had carried, and the quiver he'd had on his hip, were of an impressive quality. His aim... Well, Beah was lucky the errant arrow had merely nicked his leg and not done worse, or heat sickness would not be a concern for either of them ever again, and the rain-loving morroul would have a full belly. He'd give Eamon credit where it was due, though. The foreigner *had* killed the beast despite his physical state. His skill, plus the quality of his weapons, would mark him as a well-respected warrior in Beah's tribe. But his pale skin would keep him from ever being welcome. They were not people forgiving of *difference*.

As the shadows slid across the cave, Eamon's temperature lowered, and his body stopped quivering. When Beah trickled more water into his mouth and he swallowed without any coaxing, he felt it was safe to build a small fire. Eamon may have been suffering heat sickness, but the desert got cold at night, and the cave provided little shelter from the temperatures. Beah needed the heat. He left Eamon's side and moved to kindle a fire.

Chapter Six

RAFE

"My lord."

Rafe didn't turn around. The red sun was setting, and the last search parties had returned. It had been days, and the only sign they'd found of Eamon was a handful of arrows scattered around the beach. He didn't expect Kiran's news to be any different today than it'd been the past three nights. After the sun had disappeared below the sea, and the sky shone green and blue and purple, he turned and gave his kneeling retainer his attention.

"No luck?"

"N-no, my lord. I'm sorry."

Rafe nodded. "Dismissed."

Kiran stood but didn't leave. He gazed up at Rafe, who stood above him on the raised platform separating his bedroom from the rest of his chambers. It was only two steps up, with heavy dark curtains, which could be drawn around it for more privacy. But Rafe hadn't needed any privacy lately.

"My lord, have you fed since Eamon went missing?"

They both knew the answer, so Rafe didn't bother to respond. He had barely left his chambers; he certainly hadn't taken another human into his arms to feed.

"You must maintain your strength," Kiran advised.

The taller rin frowned at him. "Eamon is not dead."

Kiran sighed. "Perhaps not, my lord, but if he isn't dead, then I don't know where he is or why he hasn't returned, and you cannot wait for him to return before you feed again."

"He's hurt. I don't know how I know, Kiran, but I do." It wasn't a physical presence like he'd grown accustomed to—he didn't hear Eamon's thoughts or feel his emotions as if they were his own, but he *knew*. Eamon was alive and he was hurt. A dull discomfort permeated his whole body and had only been getting worse since Eamon's disappearance. His human lover needed him. But where to go or how to get there? Rafe had no sense of place from Eamon, just...life.

"You fed from unbound humans for many, many years," Kiran said. "Surely, you wouldn't rather die than return to them? If Eamon is hurt, you won't do him any favors by weakening yourself."

Rafe's stomach twisted at the thought of resorting to feeding from a different human every time he grew hungry. Yes, Kiran was right. He'd fed from hundreds, perhaps thousands of humans and other rin in his lifetime. The manor had a pool of servants and consorts who craved the feeding, and Rafe had had them all many times over. Yet it had never been *right* until he met Eamon. He and Eamon had shared something more, something he'd never found with anyone else. His bond of service with Kiran was perhaps the closest he'd ever had, but it was platonic. Kiran was a handsome rin, strong and capable, but he'd never stirred Rafe's blood like Eamon did. The thought of returning to the sickening necessity of feeding on someone he did not desire, driving them to orgasm under his hands while his body remained uninterested, made Rafe consider reverting to the taking of blood, something only the youngest of rin had to resort to. It was less...intimate.

"Can you feed from me?" Kiran asked after a pause, in a gentle voice.

Rafe's attention jerked up to his retainer's gold eyes, and he held the gaze. Slowly, Rafe descended the steps to where Kiran waited. He took Kiran's face in both hands. Feeding from another rin was possible but just as dangerous for them as it would be for a human. Perhaps all the more so, since, unlike humans, rin couldn't regenerate their own life force. Rafe focused on Kiran's eyes and slipped into his mind like fitting a hand into a glove. He saw pain there, worry, sadness...and fear. Fear that Eamon was dead and Rafe was mistaken. Fear that Rafe would let himself weaken and die in mourning for someone who'd been his bound companion for such a small fraction of his life.

Taking hold of Kiran's consciousness, Rafe backed out of his mind and pulled, drawing Kiran's awareness into his own. Under Rafe's hands, Kiran gasped. Reading his lord's mind was forbidden, even if he had the skill to carry it out in the first place. But Rafe let Kiran see inside him, how he ached, how he *knew* Eamon was alive and *knew* he was unwell. It was a certainty, as natural as he understood water was wet and fire was hot. Such knowledge came with the spiritual bond formed during the ritual Rafe and Eamon had undergone together. He let Kiran see his emptiness. Eamon was well liked in the manor by all, except a few of the aforementioned consorts and servants who were jealous he was Rafe's only companion. Well-liked didn't begin to describe Rafe's feelings though. He loved Eamon, and he desired him. He merely had to set eyes on the human, and it was impossible to think straight until he'd had the chance to put his mouth and hands all over his bare skin.

Kiran was gasping and keening, and Rafe pushed his consciousness into his own mind, separated them from each other, and stepped away. Kiran wobbled and lowered himself to his knees again. His body slouched in a dizzy stupor, and Rafe saw and smelled his arousal at his experience of Rafe's memories with Eamon. They remained silent for some time before Kiran spoke again.

"If Eamon doesn't return," he said slowly, his voice slurred as if drunk, "do you think you will survive?"

Survive? Yes, Rafe would survive. He had always survived. He hadn't gotten to this age and this position by giving up when things got tough. But he would always remember the passion and desire of these past few years with Eamon. What they did in the bedroom was fun, but Rafe's heart ached for the loss of a precious friend more than a romantic lover. He found joy and comfort in Eamon's enthusiasm and smile, his eagerness to learn and teach, his love of animals and the outdoors. In all his long life, Rafe had never met anyone who gave him such profound peace.

"I will survive," Rafe said. "I may not be happy, but I will live."

Kiran spoke softly. "I hope Eamon is well, wherever he is."

"Me too."

After the past days of fruitless searching, it seemed there were only two options for where Eamon might be: dead in the sea, or—if Rafe's intuitions were to be believed—somehow, alive in another world. If it were the latter, the chances of him making it home weren't good. Travel between worlds was limited and strictly controlled by King Soren. Seacliff was too far from the capitol to warrant interest or inclusion in such trading.

Rafe wondered if he would feel Eamon die from the other side of the universe. Would closure be worse than hope?

Chapter Seven

EAMON

The smell of cooking meat and the rumbling of his empty stomach woke Eamon. A fire crackled nearby, its heat barely grazing the side of his mostly nude body. Smooth red stone rose up on his right, curving over him like a ceiling. Vague memories flicked across his mind, of staggering up a hill, being undressed and given water by a stranger. Speaking, but he didn't remember what he'd said or what had been said to him. He twisted and saw the stranger squatting on the other side of the fire, tending to some spitted chunks of meat. Smoke rose toward the ceiling and seemed to travel along the stone and out a crack near the back wall. Sunlight lay on the floor near the cave entrance, and Eamon wondered how long he'd been asleep.

The person's head was uncovered. Eamon took a moment to stare now that his mind was clearer. The stranger's brown skin was smooth, with soft features and a small mouth, dark eyes, and dark hair. Young, barely out of teenage years if Eamon had to guess, and feminine, but with a jagged, short haircut similar to Eamon's own.

"You're awake," the stranger said, and Eamon jumped guiltily when he realized he'd been staring.

"Yes."

"Do you remember what happened?" Their voice was gentle and high, and they spoke slowly. Caddenese lay buried in Eamon's mind, dusty with disuse, and he was grateful for his rescuer's slow cadence. Occasionally, he encountered a book in Rafe's library written in Caddenese and got to practice the old language, but reading and speaking were two different skills.

"Yes. Some."

"You saved me. I saved you. My name is Beah."

Despite their feminine appearance and voice, the stranger used masculine language, and the name was masculine. If his Caddenese served him...and he wasn't so sure it had yet.

"I'm Eamon," he said, and then, cautiously, "You use male language?"

"Yes." Simple. No explanation or defense. Beah held his gaze with an expression of defiance, *daring* Eamon to make a comment about his whiskerless cheeks or long lashes. Eamon didn't. He smiled.

"Thank you for saving me, Master Beah."

Shoulders now relaxed, Beah reached out to poke at the fire with a charred piece of wood. "How do you feel?"

Eamon took stock of his body for a second before answering. His arms and face didn't hurt as bad as they had been since the first day, but his mouth was dry, his head ached, and his back was sore from sleeping on stone. Every inch of his skin was grimy and sand-coated, and he would have done a lot of embarrassing things in exchange for a long, hot bath. But overall, he figured he could have been worse. At least he wasn't panicking.

"Alive," Eamon said finally. His voice croaked over a dry throat.

Beah snorted and pointed two fingers at the waterskin at Eamon's side. "Drink."

"Thank you."

Some of the dizziness had cleared out of his head while he slept, but it would take more than a nap to recover his strength, and his hands shook with the weight of the full waterskin. Water spilled out the corner of his mouth and left a cool trail over his burnt skin. He wanted to drown himself in it, he was so thirsty, but he remembered vomiting at least once before falling asleep, and lowered the waterskin to his lap.

"I rescued your arrows," Beah said, gesturing over Eamon's shoulder to where his quiver leaned on the wall. All five arrows were in place, and Eamon felt relief over something he hadn't even known he was worried about. His bow was there, too, miraculously still intact.

"Thank you."

Meat cooked over an open flame had never smelled so good, and Eamon scooted closer to the fire to watch it spit and sizzle. There were two large chunks impaled on sharpened sticks, one for each of them. His stomach growled again, loudly, and Beah took one of the spitted pieces of meat off the fire, inspected it, and then offered it to Eamon like a weapon, aiming the sharp end toward himself. Eamon accepted with a gracious nod.

"Thank you."

"It's hot," Beah said. "Eat slowly."

Eamon blew on the cooked chunk of flesh, bracing his elbows on his legs to help support the weight of the stick and its delicious-smelling burden. He was willing to risk burning his mouth for the joy of having fresh food in his stomach, but he waited for his host to take a bite before he followed suit. The meat flaked off in large chunks, similar to most kinds of fowl, and he hummed in appreciation.

For a while, nothing was more important than filling his stomach, and they ate in companionable silence across the fire from each other. After the meat was gone, Beah offered him a bowl of what appeared to be greenish fruit, and Eamon took a piece and bit into the sweet flesh. Where had the stranger found so much food when Eamon hadn't seen anything edible for miles?

"What is this?" he asked, gesturing at the stick holding his meat and the fruit he had in his hand.

"Opuntia," Beah said, gesturing at the fruit, "and...morroul. It's fresh."

The words were unfamiliar, but Eamon nodded and tried to commit them to memory so he could ask about how to acquire more opuntia and morroul if the need arose.

While they ate, the spot of sunlight on the stone floor shortened and then disappeared altogether. The flames cast dancing shadows over Beah, like a frantic crash and ebb of dark waves on the expanse of loose fabric he wore draped about him. Orange sparks glowed in his dark eyes, and though his face held no expression, something about him seemed sad. Eamon suppressed a shiver. The air drifting in through the narrow cave mouth had grown cold with the coming of night, and Eamon pulled his cloak on and scooted nearer the fire. His movement seemed to remind Beah he was there, and he blinked out of his reverie and looked across the fire at Eamon.

"Where are you from?"

Eamon sorted through his memory for the right words. He wasn't sure he'd know how to answer even if they were both fluent in the same language. He finally settled on a simple phrase that expressed a lot of information. "Another world."

Beah's eyes narrowed. "Another world?"

His skepticism made Eamon wonder if he hadn't phrased it right, but he nodded and hoped for the best. "I fell through a..." He struggled for words. Back home they were called gates or portals, but he couldn't pull the Caddenese word from his groggy mind. "A hole? A tear? Fighting a..." The word for ghoul failed him, and he mimed the fight they'd had that morning.

"Morroul."

The word sounded far too similar to what they'd just eaten. Eamon's full belly twisted. "Morroul?" And he pointed at the sharpened stick he'd eaten from. A flash of something—guilt?—crossed Beah's face, but he nodded, and Eamon swallowed and mimed shooting his bow. "Morroul?"

"Yes. The same."

Oh, gods, he'd just eaten *ghoul*? It had been delicious! But the thought of what they fed on made his stomach turn as if he'd just eaten a writhing glob of maggots. Had it had human meat in its belly, in its blood? The food turned sour in his stomach, but he did his best to hide his disgust. Apparently, not well enough.

"The gods will forgive us," Beah said. "It wasn't our time to die, or the morroul would have taken us."

The words made sense, but the meaning was lost. What did the gods have to do with anything?

"I-I...Ghouls—morroul—they're...foul."

Beah's face betrayed nothing. It was so still it had to be hiding some other reaction. "Do you not believe morroul are servants of the gods?"

At first, Eamon was sure he'd misunderstood and repeated the phrase back to his companion, who nodded. Servants of the gods? *Servants of the gods?* Eamon had seen Rafe treat storeroom vermin with more respect than he treated ghouls. They were further from the gods than the lowliest of insects, the most destructive of rodents. He remembered Rafe's cold fury from their first encounter with a ghoul, the rage at the creature's audacity to trespass where it was not welcome.

But he didn't have enough words to express those things.

"No," Eamon said finally. "Where I come from, they are...not considered such."

"But you know them? They are in your...world?"

"Yes, but they...invade. They are not welcome."

Beah nodded, brow furrowed in thought. "In my village, they are worshipped." For the first time since Eamon had met Beah, the other man smiled. It was a vicious expression, full of bitterness. "The priests would die if they knew I just ate one."

Clearly, there was no love lost between Beah and his village's holy men. Eamon identified with the feeling, but he was more interested in the first part of Beah's statement. *In my village...* There were villages here. There were other people, communities. There was hope.

"You said you came through a 'tear' to get here," Beah said. "Are there many of these tears?"

"No. The ghoul made it. I don't know how, but they come into my world." Until a few years ago, it was believed only humans had the magic necessary to travel between worlds with ease. Rin didn't. It was a shock that ghouls did, but there was no other explanation for them coming through.

Beah's voice was low when he replied. "My mother would say death comes to all worlds."

Death. Yes, the ghouls certainly brought death. Maybe they were servants of the gods, and Eamon had been chosen to die. Maybe he was actually in the afterlife now. He hadn't done anything bad enough in his life to deserve this kind of suffering.

"Why couldn't you go back?" Beah asked.

"The tear was gone."

Beah's brow furrowed again. They lapsed into silence.

There in the small cave, across from another human being, it was easy to forget he was on another world instead of just camping, as he'd done hundreds of times in his life. Nothing about Beah marked him as foreign or strange, and inside the cave at night, it was easy to forget the two suns. The familiarity of the crackling fire lulled Eamon into a serene confidence. He had a full belly, water, shelter, fire, and company. Tomorrow...tomorrow he would...what? Go skipping merrily home to Rafe?

"Have you ever seen, uh, morroul make tears?" he asked.

"No."

"Have you ever seen *anyone* make tears?"

Beah shook his head, and Eamon deflated.

"Where were you trying to go, walking through the desert?" Beah asked.

"Home. Back to my world. I need to go home. I am..." Words failed him—the rite of bondage between a rin and their human companion was from rin culture, and, as such, there was no perfectly equivalent Caddenese word. Eamon settled for, "Married."

Beah nodded, calm, as if he'd expected the answer. "Children?"

"No," Eamon said quickly. "No, no children."

Beah nodded again and returned his gaze to the fire.

Eamon pressed his lips together, wanting to ask more questions but unsure how far to push his host. Unsure how much more information he could take in one night. The fire crackled between them, and Eamon held his hands out to the heat. It stung his injured arms, and he jerked away, tears springing to his eyes at the surprising intensity.

Beah rose in a swirl of brown robes, strode to the back wall, and returned with a clay jar of green salve. He sat on Eamon's right, took a generous helping of goo on three fingers, and smeared it along Eamon's bicep. When the pain dulled immediately, Eamon let out a soft noise of relief. Beah offered him the jar to continue the treatment himself.

"Thank you." Eamon applied it with his forefingers, rubbing it across blisters and tight, flaky areas with extra care. It numbed the fingers he was using, but he didn't mind the trade-off.

"Tell me about your world." Beah's voice was slow and contemplative, and Eamon looked across the fire at him. He didn't know the other man well enough to determine where his train of thought was going, but he nodded. How did one give a description of an entire world, especially if he'd only seen parts of it?

After a second, he smiled to himself.

"'Sunless skies stretch sea to sea, life is lush but warmth is not, yet beings like humans thrive...'"

At Beah's confused expression, Eamon shook his head and smiled. "It's from a book. I didn't translate it well, maybe."

"You have no sun?"

"We have a sun. Just one, and where I live, it's hardly ever visible. It's nothing like this." He gestured vaguely toward the entrance of the cave. Beah continued to look perplexed, but curiosity lay in the furrowed brow and narrowed eyes.

"We live together with rin," Eamon said and then suddenly wondered, "Do you have rin here?"

The confusion remained. "I don't know what a 'rin' is."

"Oh. Um." Eamon stared thoughtfully at the shimmering ointment on his arm, if only for something to focus on other than Beah's face. "They're people like humans, but not. They're stronger. Older."

Confusion turned to suspicion. "Do they eat humans too?"

"W-well, in a way…"

"They are dangerous, then? Like morroul."

"No! No, they're nothing like morroul." He didn't know how to explain it to Beah. It was hard to explain even with a shared fluency in language. Many humans in his world *still* didn't understand or accept living in peace with beings who, for all intents and purposes, were their natural predators. "They only take what they need. Small…drinks."

"Of blood?"

Beah looked so suspicious, Eamon was afraid he was about to be thrown out of the cave and told to never come back. Beah *did* speak the Caddenese language. Perhaps he had similar beliefs to those in the closed human-only communities Eamon had grown up in. When he hesitated to answer, Beah spoke again.

"We tell our children stories about blood drinkers to keep them in their beds at night. I thought they were not real. Who is your deity?"

Eamon frowned, startled by the sharp tone of his companion's voice. Rin, not real? Children's stories? Eamon had never been to other worlds, but he knew dragons and wizards and fae were not mere children's stories. Even as a child, he'd known ghouls were real too. How had they come to believe such a thing?

"Our deity is Shadelin," Beah said when Eamon still didn't answer. Despite his suspicion, he seemed eager for conversation, and Eamon didn't blame him. He lived in a cave. "The morroul are his servants, if you believe such things."

So Beah shared aspects of Eamon's childhood religion. Shadelin was the deity of death, fear, and sleepless nights, an unpleasant specter in any and all imaginings Eamon had ever seen. Ghouls being servants of Shadelin made sense, in a morbid way. In his youth, Eamon had laid out offerings to the shapeless dark entity and prayed for relief from the unexplained panic that gripped him so often. Surely, the god of fear might make fear go away as easily as he might provoke it? Over fifteen years later, the fear still came. Eamon didn't have much faith in the gods these days.

"My family honored the goddess Wesige, the hunter."

Beah's brows rose. "You came so far!"

Eamon shook his head. It was clear they had some shared tenets in their religions, but they were not identical. Beah's statement meant nothing to Eamon in relation to Wesige. They might stay awake and debate religion all night, or he could try to learn more.

"So you know there are other worlds."

"Of course."

"But no one goes to them?"

"No. No one can."

"Not even royalty? Traders? Merchants?"

Beah's chuckle was sardonic. "No one leaves the village. No one leaves this world. It is forbidden by the gods."

Eamon replaced the lid on the jar of salve but didn't pass it back to his companion. None of what he'd said sounded good. None of it was what Eamon wanted to hear. Despair pressed into his throat and chest, making it hard to breathe.

Since falling into this world, he'd been nothing but a bundle of pain and fear. Eamon was well acquainted with fear—the type of fear that came to him for no reason, unexpected and unprovoked, and set his heart racing and his hands shaking with a baseless conviction of oncoming death. Rafe would sit with him through the panic but didn't touch him, because that would make it worse. Fear had been his constant companion since childhood. *This* fear, this despair, was different. For once, being afraid he might die was justified. Being afraid he might never see his lover again was a real possibility. The sick feelings, the pain, had been physical and not in his head.

Out of nowhere, the reality of his situation caught up to him. His goal had been to reach the mountains, and now here he was. So what next? Did it matter? Was there even a way for him to get home? How far was he going to make it with ghouls prowling around? Some of those creatures were as big as a house. Even a runt was dangerous enough to do serious damage if it got a hold of him. He had a few arrows and a knife. And even supposing he did survive the ghouls, where would he go? No one left the village, no one left the world? There had to be a way to get from this world back to his own—the ghouls had been doing it regularly for years. But what were the chances any human knew? Humans didn't come through. Only ghouls. Gods, he was going to be stuck here forever.

He got up and headed for the front of the cave.

"Where are you going?" Beah asked.

"I can't breathe."

The cave entrance was narrow, and Eamon would have to turn sideways to fit through. How in the worlds had Beah gotten him in here? It wasn't a long tunnel, but he still hesitated, and his host appeared beside him so suddenly he jumped. He hadn't heard Beah get up.

"Are you unwell?"

Eamon's resolve to get out of the cave crumbled and he leaned on the stone, resting his forehead against it. Here came the familiar shakes, the nausea, the cold sweats, and this time, he didn't have Rafe there with him. The last time he'd been without his lover during a breakdown, he'd been barely more than a kid, travelling out into the big scary world for the first time. That realization just made it worse, and his eyes stung. He swore.

"Eamon," Beah said. "What is it?"

His voice came out strained with the effort of not breaking down crying. "I'm going to die here."

The other man didn't rush forth with reassurances, and Eamon groaned. Beah hadn't reassured him, because he knew damn well it was true. Maybe not today, maybe not tomorrow, but someday.

He was stuck here now. This was where he would die.

Chapter Eight

EAMON

"Do you know anyone who has ever...left?"

They walked side by side, cloaked and hooded against the sun. For three days, Eamon had been regaining his strength and nagging his host for details about the environment and the world. That day, they were harvesting opuntia, the fruit-like growths of cacti, and the long leaves of the shade-loving cacti which produced the healing green goo Eamon had been applying to his sunburn. Eamon hadn't been eager to wander around in the sunlight again after nearly dying in it, but Beah explained how foolish he'd been to leave his skin exposed all day—the sun back home was not so hot, the days not so long—and he'd forced himself to leave the cave. He couldn't hide there forever.

Beah was companionable enough, with a childlike curiosity about Eamon's world, but not forthcoming with personal details of his own. He wouldn't tell Eamon why he was alone out here, but he shared stories about the village where he'd grown up, how they acquired water, how they grew crops and raised livestock. The village was all he knew. There were stories of sprawling utopias in other parts of the world, but the desert didn't house the resources necessary to sustain much life. The village Beah had lived in until recently worshipped the twelve—similar gods to those Eamon had grown up kneeling to in his family's tiny altar room—and took their beliefs very seriously.

"It is against the laws to leave the village," Beah said after such a long time Eamon had to think to recall his question. And for another moment, that was all Beah said. Eamon was about to push him for more when he continued. "Any who do will be struck down by the gods, and a plague put upon the village. It is the will of the gods we remain in our places and serve them to the best of our ability. So they say."

"They?"

"The elders. The holy men." Beah paused. "Yet, I've been away longer than anyone else ever has been, and I'm still alive."

"I left my village when I turned seventeen," Eamon said. "I have been away for over ten years, and I am still alive." No one had told him the gods would strike him down simply for leaving when he did, but his parents had suspected he intended to go do "ungodly" things with bloodsucking monsters. *That* he would be struck down for. So they said.

Beah knelt at the base of a cliff, and Eamon stepped around him to watch as he deftly carved the fruit off another cactus and dropped it in a bag he carried at his waist. These fruits would be a welcome treat in their diet of dried ghoul meat and tepid water. Accustomed to certain luxuries after so many years living with Rafe, Eamon struggled to adapt to this bare-bones fare, but it kept strength in his body, and he knew he needed that.

"So you've never known anyone who left the village?"

"No."

"What about you?"

Beah said nothing. Silence was his answer to any question about personal things.

"What about people from other villages? Has anyone ever come *to* your village?"

The other man straightened and looked up at Eamon. "Two," he said.

Two. Eamon tried to imagine only meeting two new people in his entire life. It was unfathomable to him.

"A man I met once in my youth said he'd been to other worlds. He stayed in my village a short time and wanted me to leave with him when he went."

The mention of other worlds made Eamon's heart rate spike.

"What other worlds? How did he get there? Did he create the tears himself?"

Back home, there were humans in employ of the king who were able to create gates. They were rare and highly valued—but if a few humans here and there had the ability, surely there had to be others not in King Soren's employ who had it. Humans from other worlds.

"Yes," Beah said softly. His eyes turned off into the distance, and Eamon followed his gaze to see if he was actually looking at something. All he saw was dusty red rock.

"Where was he going?"

Beah shrugged. "Somewhere far away. Far from this death pit."

"Why didn't you go with him?"

Beah shook his head. "Leaving the village is forbidden. Leaving the world can only be worse."

"Oh."

They started walking again, Beah in the lead. Eamon waited until they'd crested a rise and began traipsing down into a narrow canyon before he spoke again, a little breathless.

"What about the second person?"

"What?"

"You said two people had come to your village."

"Oh. An herbalist. She did not stay long either." Beah hopped off a short ledge and turned to offer Eamon a hand. Eamon smiled at the gesture from the smaller, younger person, but accepted it in good spirits and hopped down. They'd descended into a shadowed area full of the sun cure plant, and Beah handed Eamon a small knife so they'd make faster progress harvesting it. Conversation lapsed as they worked.

On the way back to their small shelter, Eamon broke the silence.

"Can you take me to your village?"

Without hesitation or so much as a glance over his shoulder, Beah said, "No."

Fear struck Eamon and gave him a boost of speed to catch up to his companion. "Why not?"

Beah shook his head. They were near the cave, and Eamon wasn't certain he wanted to sleep in that small space for another night if he had no hope of getting home. It would be suffocating. He grabbed Beah's arm, forcing him to stop, but Beah didn't turn to face him.

"Please," Eamon said. "I have to at least *try* to get home. I can't stay here forever. I can't die here."

"I cannot return there." He jerked his arm out of Eamon's grip and began walking again. The fear grew stronger in Eamon's chest and he hurried to keep up with Beah's determined strides.

"*Please,*" he said again. "Take me there. Come with me. I can reward you when I get home. I have access to money. Goods. Livestock. Weapons. I'll get you anything you want. Please."

"I said I cannot," Beah snapped, spinning on his heel to face Eamon. He held his body tense, hands clenched into fists as he glared. "That doesn't mean I don't *want* to go back; it means I *cannot*, Eamon. I'm not welcome there. Do you think I would be living in a cave alone if I had a home?"

It was the closest Beah had come to disclosing something personal. Eamon barely hesitated before pushing. "Why can't you?"

Beah shook his head, turned, and continued down the path.

Typical. Perhaps if Eamon opened up first, Beah would feel more comfortable. Or at the very least, perhaps he would feel pity.

"Please," Eamon said again. They were heading up the slope toward where they'd first met. The stench of rotting flesh and punctured bowels suffocated him, and Eamon pulled his cloak up to cover his nose and mouth as he spoke. Words burbled out of him, and he wasn't even sure what language he was speaking anymore. "My husband's name is Rafe. We've been together for over ten years. For over ten years, I'm the only human he has fed from, and he is the only rin I've allowed to feed from me. He watches out for me, and I for him. We fight side by side. We sleep side by side. He is the lord of Seacliff Manor."

"None of this means anything to me," Beah returned, and both of them had to fall silent and hold their breaths as they edged past the remains of the ghoul. A handful of carrion eaters and scavengers paused to give the two travelers wary, dangerous glares. They continued on heedless of their animal audience, trying not to smell the rot. Only once they had traveled a sufficient distance did Eamon continue speaking.

"I'm sick," he confessed as his heart raced from exertion and anxiety. "I have bouts of terrible, suffocating fear and anger, and I cannot control them. They make it difficult to do anything. They've been getting worse lately. Rafe helps me get through them. I need him as much as he needs me. Please, Beah."

Beah pushed into the narrow crevice leading into the cave they'd been sharing, and Eamon followed. He'd been getting more accustomed to squeezing through the entrance, but he still hated it.

"Can you help me get to your village but not actually go into it?" he asked as Beah unloaded his pack and the pouch from his belt. "Take me there and then leave, come back here?"

"No."

Eamon stared at Beah's shoulders as the man shuffled around at the rear of the cave. What else was there to say or do? He couldn't stay here. There was no life for him here. He had to try every possibility before he gave up, no matter how often he broke down into panics at the mere thought of doing something so dangerous. Maybe someone else in the village would know more. Beah was barely more than a kid. If Eamon had to talk to every single person in the village to find out a way to get home, he would.

"If you won't take me there, then tell me how to get there on my own," he said, resigned.

Beah glanced over his shoulder, face still hidden. "I can do that," he said, "but it's a long journey, and dangerous. It's not wise to go alone."

"You're not giving me much choice," Eamon snapped. "What am I supposed to do, live in this cave with you forever?"

With his back turned, it was impossible to tell how Beah reacted, but his voice was soft after a pause. "No, I suppose not."

"You made it here. I can make it there. I can't stay here and wait to die. Rafe might think I'm already dead for all I know, and I can't stand the thought of him hurting needlessly. I love him."

Only the faint rustle of Beah's clothes interrupted the following silence. When it became evident he was not going to speak, Eamon considered the discussion ended and went to sit by the wall.

His heart would not stop racing, and he was angry. He couldn't tell if the anger was justified or merely a side effect of the fear, but he wanted it to go away. *Anger does not suit you,* Rafe had said once, after enduring an outburst of panic-fueled irrational fury. It was true. Eamon hated anger. He hated the uncontrollable rage, knowing it was unnecessary but not how to stop it. It would ebb as he calmed, and he'd be left with regret and shame at the things he said or did under its influence. As much as he wanted to let it out in a blistering tirade, his best move was holding his tongue—literally, if need be.

He didn't speak again as his host went about starting a fire and putting together a small meal for them. He accepted the food with thanks, but they did not converse as they ate. Silence in itself wasn't unusual, but this time, it was tinged with discomfort and tension Eamon did not like. Still, he couldn't apologize or change his mind to comfort his host. He had to try everything to get back home. If Beah was lonely, he was welcome to travel with him.

A terrible idea struck him for the first time since his arrival at least a week ago. What if Rose, Tuomas, and Lionel were dead? Or what if they'd been thrown through a tear, too, but ended up somewhere different? Gods, they were fools. He should have accepted Rafe's offer of an escort. Maybe if he wasn't so stubborn, he'd be at home in bed right now.

And Rafe...well, the downside of being a creature that thrived on energy from other living things meant he'd have to start taking from someone else. After feeding exclusively from Eamon for so long, now he would have to lay hands on a stranger.

For most rin, feeding was enjoyable. They had humans throwing themselves at their feet for a chance at the addictive pleasure they elicited during feeding. Sex, or at least physical intimacy, was rote. Most didn't give it a second thought.

Rafe gave it a second thought, and a third, and a fourth. The pleasure and feeding were tinged with inexplicable discomfort. Except with Eamon. They'd been inside each other's minds, so it was clear to Eamon how Rafe had felt those many times he'd bedded strangers—people he didn't love, people he wasn't attracted to—out of necessity.

Eamon's appetite left him at the memory of Rafe's discomfort, and he offered the crude clay bowl back to Beah, cactus fruits untouched. "Thank you," he said again, as Beah accepted the bowl with a confused expression on his face. "I'm going to retire early. I should leave in the morning."

Beah's expression grew tense, but he nodded and said nothing else.

Chapter Nine

BEAH

For a long time after Eamon fell asleep, Beah watched him. The pale man's burns had healed considerably over the past few days of treatment and rest, and Beah had another jar of the salve he would send off with him in the morning. He had water, and once he got to the forest, water would not be such a rare commodity anymore. Eamon's biggest concern would be surviving the wildlife.

He liked Eamon though. In these days together, Eamon hadn't questioned him about things such as why he didn't have stubble on his cheeks, or why he was of such small stature or had such a high voice for a man. Beah, for the first time ever, felt comfortable with himself in another person's presence. Other questions had come in spades, but the one thing Beah feared, the one thing so many of his family and friends didn't even try to get right, this stranger had never once stumbled over.

Perhaps where he came from, it was common for men's souls to be born into soft bodies with breasts and wide hips. In Beah's village, such things were not common, and no matter how he insisted he was not meant for womanly things, they refused to see past his body. *It is a woman's role to bring new lives into this world*, he'd been told a thousand times by a dozen different voices. Once, when he broke down and told his mother he was not a woman, she scowled at him. *This is the body your gods have given you, and it is the body you must use to serve them. Your body is suited for womanly things. You must find a husband.*

Afterward, things had only gotten worse. As much as he liked Eamon and didn't want him to die, Beah could not return there. He was supposed to be dead. Their first attempt hadn't succeeded. If he returned, he doubted their second attempt would leave room for error. Eamon was a skilled archer, born on the hunter deity's world. If anyone had a chance at surviving the journey, he did—at least, once he got out of the desert.

As quietly as possible, Beah put together a pack for Eamon. Dried meat and some dried fruit. An extra waterskin. A jar of the sun cure salve. A blanket. It wasn't much, but it was the best he had to offer without putting his own well-being at risk. That done, he curled up on the stone near the fire and attempted to sleep. It took a long time to claim him.

DAWN WOKE HIM. Even before a single ray of light fell through the cave entrance, he was awake and moving. Eamon rolled over and blinked a few times, watching Beah stoke the fire back to life.

"Good morning," Eamon said.

"Morning. Did you sleep well?"

"No." He sat up and stretched, warming and loosening his muscles. Beah watched. Eamon's arms and legs were well muscled, his pale skin oddly beautiful even with its extensive peeling burns. Though it did nothing for him sexually or intimately, Beah still enjoyed the company of another person. He would regret losing it, but he couldn't hold Eamon back.

"I will take you to the edge of the forest," Beah said. "Are you hungry?"

Eamon hesitated and then nodded. Beah felt a strange joy—preparing and eating a small meal would give them more time together. Though he was content in solitude, it was nice to hear a voice other than his own on occasion. He would miss Eamon.

"How far away is the forest?"

"A day's walk, if we're efficient. There is a pass through the mountains which will save time."

"Why do you stay here if the forest is so near? I can't imagine this is better."

"I am desert born and mountain raised," Beah said. "The forest is more dangerous and less familiar to me."

"Oh." Eamon smiled a little. "I'm forest born and forest raised. I'll be all right."

Some of the tension in Beah's chest released. He smiled. "I'm glad."

They ate in silence. Beah wanted to say something, to explain or apologize to this stranger for sending him on his way with no guide, but the right words never came to him. Instead, he waited for Eamon to finish, then grabbed the pack he'd put together for him.

"Some supplies," he said, standing to offer it to his guest. Eamon stood, hesitated, and then bowed as he accepted it.

"Thank you." He paused and then said, "You could come with me."

"Eamon..."

"I mean come back home with me. Back to Seacliff Manor."

Beah bit his lip to keep himself from saying, "*If* you make it." There was one person in Beah's village who might be able to help Eamon, but if Beah gave her up, she would know. Worse, if Eamon said the wrong thing to the wrong person in the village, it would end with him and Alma both in the pit.

"I have lived my lives. My next adventure is the afterlife," Beah said. "I have no place in Wesige's world."

"Everyone is welcome," Eamon said, his voice rising with a hint of desperation. "You could work in the manor or serve in the guard. When I tell Rafe you saved my life, you'll be able to do whatever you want. He would give you lands, if you want. A house."

Lands and a house were the last things Beah wanted. He just wanted to be left alone. Maybe Eamon's lover would give him a house in the woods where no one would bother him. No one would remark on his *beauty*, and the village boys wouldn't make comments about his chest. No one would laugh in his face when he asked to take part in the men's coming of age ceremony. No one would try to force anything on him.

But...he had as much here. And there were a lot of "ifs" involved in that scenario. He'd only be able to go with Eamon to his world if they both survived the trip to the village. If the elders didn't have him killed or arrested on sight. If Alma actually created tears to other worlds, as he suspected. If she would get them both to where they wanted to go.

No. Too many ifs. He'd made it this far. Backtracking wasn't an option.

"I'm sorry, Eamon. I can't."

The other man's jaw tightened, and he looked down but tried to disguise his disappointment with a quick smile. "Your loss."

Beah smiled. "I suppose it is."

He put out the fire, covered it, tucked the few belongings he would not be bringing with him into a small nook at the back of the cave and strapped on his sword belt. He was comforted by its presence, even if he wasn't very good at using it.

They set out with Beah in the lead, both cloaked, hooded, and armed. The pass leading to the forest would take half a day to reach, and from there, another half day to traverse. On the other side, they'd have to descend into the trees, and Beah would leave Eamon at the river. It would take him all the way to the village if he followed it closely.

For most of the morning, they remained silent, focused on keeping their footing on the uneven ground. In the mountains, the heat was slightly more bearable than on the desert flats, but even so, Eamon seemed to struggle. Beah took pity on him after a few hours and found a place to pause and rest their legs. He remained standing, but Eamon found an outcropping of rock to climb up and sit on with his legs dangling over the edge, childlike.

"Are there deserts where you're from?" Beah asked after they'd caught their breath.

Eamon smiled. "There are, but I live by the sea." His voice had a wistful tone to it. "The manor house is on a high cliff. You can see everything from there. Down the hill a ways, there's a village. Everything is lush and green, there are trees and flowers and rivers and streams. The sky is a deep blue, and we only have one sun which never rises as high as the suns here do." He squinted at the orange sky above them, face screwed up in a scowl.

It sounded like a fantastical wonderland to Beah. He'd never even heard of a "sea," and asked Eamon to clarify the word. Eamon's expression turned to shock, and then he seemed to think about it, shrug, and accept Beah's lack of understanding. He gestured to the desert behind them, visible through the opening of the shallow canyon they now stood in. It stretched out forever, until the dusty orange-brown of the ground disappeared into the hazy orange of the sky.

"Imagine if that was all water," Eamon said. "Then it would be a sea."

Beah's eyes widened, and he looked out at the desert again, forcing his mind to convert the orange-brown to a blue-green and the ripples of heat haze to shimmering sparkles of light on water. It seemed impossible, but he had heard of such places in legends. Water so deep, one would never find a place to touch the bottom. Water rife with scaled monstrosities and mysteries no one would ever understand.

"What lives there?" Beah asked.

"In the sea?" Eamon shrugged. "Fish, I suppose. Lobsters. Serpents."

Fish! Beah had seen a living fish for the first time only recently. The stream he'd been following from the mountains to the river had widened into a sluggish pool under the low-hanging boughs of a tree. The fish had been blueish and long, and their large, lidless black eyes had unnerved him even as he stared in wonder.

"The sunsets are the best," Eamon continued, staring through the canyon at the sea of gray-red rock, but Beah knew he was seeing something in his mind or memories. "I used to live farther inland, south, where the sun rose higher and the days were longer, and the sunsets were beautiful there, too, but nothing compares to the sun setting over the water."

His smile was bright, awed, happy, and his love and excitement clear to Beah. Then, just as quickly, the smile faded and Eamon looked down.

"I hope I'll get to see them again."

"You will." Beah reached up and squeezed Eamon's leg in what he hoped was a comforting gesture. "You will see many more sunsets over the sea. You will make it back to your husband. I have faith."

"That makes one of us," Eamon muttered. He hopped down off the outcropping. "Let's keep going."

Chapter Ten

RAFE

People were talking. It had been over a week, and Rafe hadn't made an announcement regarding his bound companion's disappearance. The household was aware something was wrong. Eamon hadn't been seen since leaving with his bow and arrows and three human friends, but no one knew if he was alive or dead, or if Rafe had had any role in his disappearance. Surely, they hadn't absolved their bond?

Something was afoot. Scouts came and went at all hours of the day. The stable workers had orders to prepare a small mounted contingent at a moment's notice. Extra supplies filled the larder, and the village blacksmith worked on a strange commission from the manor lord himself.

Perhaps the biggest curiosity was that Rafe had not fed on a new human in all this time. Secrets spread among servants like a bad case of the itch. If he had fed from one of them, all would have heard about it.

But he hadn't.

So people were talking.

"Let them talk," Rafe said.

"Of course, my lord," Kiran answered. He stood trembling in his lord's hands, naked and weak. Feeding from another rin wasn't common behavior, but Rafe couldn't bring himself to go back to feeding for the sake of feeding, not after the intimacy he'd shared with Eamon. Kiran was his closest companion, and though he wasn't romantically or sexually drawn to him as he was with Eamon, he loved him all the same. Bringing Kiran pleasure through feeding was more bearable than it would have been with anyone else. And Rafe had to admit seeing his loyal, flirtatious retainer shudder and moan through an orgasm under his hands had a certain appeal.

Stronger and more satisfied, Rafe eased Kiran down to the bed and fetched a rag to clean him up.

"Is the blacksmith's project complete?"

Talking about business matters through the feeding helped keep the intimate contact from getting too intimate. Kiran didn't have the same reservations as Rafe, and Rafe didn't want to lead him on. The intimacy of feeding could be, and often was, misconstrued.

"Kiran," Rafe prompted sharply, and the other rin jumped.

"Yes," he said, shaking his head to escape the post-orgasm cloud. "Yes, my lord. He's due to deliver it today." Kiran sat up and began looking for his clothes.

There were other less sexual ways to feed—drinking blood being the most prevalent—but Rafe was old enough and skilled enough to take what he needed without leaving a mark on his partner. The idea of taking blood, of physically damaging his partner, offended his sense of pride. Only young or weak rin needed blood from their partners, and he was neither. Even if he lost everything else in his life, he refused to lose his pride. And so he fed, intimate and uncomfortable as it may be.

"Very good." Rafe passed Kiran his trousers, and the other rin smiled a thanks. "Go feed yourself while I check on everything."

Kiran sat on the bed, holding his clothes but not putting them on. His dark hands clenched in the white silk of his tunic, and he stared at them, head bowed. "May I speak freely, my lord?"

That was never a good sign. Kiran was a good retainer, loyal to a fault. If he wanted to speak without the restrictions of a master/servant relationship, he didn't have anything good to say. And yet Rafe nodded. "Go ahead, my friend."

It took the other rin a moment to gather himself, to gather the courage necessary to speak.

"My lord," he said slowly. "I am not certain hunting a ghoul is a wise choice."

Rafe sighed, tired of the protests. Since bringing up the idea, protests were all he heard. "It is the only choice I have at the present moment."

There were humans who were able to create rifts between worlds—gatekeepers—but they were rare, and most were in the king's service. Any human who discovered they had gatekeeping abilities simply had to show up at the palace and they'd have their every need met for the rest of their lives as long as they pledged loyalty to King Soren. Needless to say, it was the path most gatekeepers chose. Commoners, and low-ranking lords like Rafe, were not privy to the king's dealings. He controlled commerce between worlds, choosing when gatekeepers were allowed to open portals, and to where.

Hundreds of years ago, it had been a free-for-all. Gatekeepers for hire in every major city, travel between worlds as common as travel between villages. But when humans realized they didn't have the power, even en masse, to defend themselves against all the things in the worlds that thought them tasty, they staged a purge. Non-magic humans rounded up those with the ability to tear the veil to other worlds. But the magic users rallied, left, and sealed themselves off from the other worlds, leaving some of their own kind behind, stranding rin—and likely every other sentient life-form—all over the faces of the many worlds.

Gatekeepers had only recently begun cropping up again, and travel between worlds was closely monitored. Rafe doubted a king would take any interest in mounting a rescue mission to another world for one random human. He'd send a messenger to the king as the last resort if capturing a ghoul didn't get him what he wanted.

"You don't even know where Eamon *is* if this does work!" Kiran was protesting. Rafe shook his head. They'd already had this discussion.

"He is in Shadelin. Where else would he go, if a ghoul cast him from one world to another? It's the only logical answer."

"All right," Kiran conceded, "but it's still an entire world. Worlds are big."

"Tears allow instantaneous travel. Once I am able to create them, it will not matter how far away he is."

"You don't know how to speak to a ghoul. They don't speak our language."

"Let me worry about that."

Kiran let out a frustrated huff of breath and got up. He tossed his clothes onto the bed as he approached Rafe. "My lord—please. Your people are worried about you."

Rafe frowned down at his retainer. "I must do this, Kiran. I can't move forward until I've exhausted every option to get him back."

"Even assuming you can find a ghoul and capture it, what can you offer to get it to obey?"

"An end to its suffering." Rafe gave Kiran a look that clearly said he would be the cause of such suffering, and Kiran swallowed. "If you would like to stay behind, merely tell me, and I will make other arrangements for my feeding during the trip."

"No," Kiran said quickly. There was no room for negotiation or argument in his faithful retainer's voice. He wasn't surprised that Kiran would be determined to serve as his substitute companion if Eamon was truly gone. "I will come with you, my lord. I would follow you into the sea if you asked. But I hate to see you torture yourself like this, and there are many others who feel the same."

"*Not* doing this would be torture," Rafe said, reaching up to cup Kiran's cheek in his palm, his skin pale in comparison to Kiran's. The same gesture made with Eamon would have him marveling at how dark he was against his lover's fair complexion. "I have been alive for roughly two hundred years, Kiran, and I have never loved or desired another the way I do Eamon. It would be a disservice to him to do anything less." He leaned in and pressed a kiss against Kiran's forehead. "I would do the same for you. If I felt certain you were not lost."

The younger rin bowed his head and pressed his cheek into his lord's touch, nuzzling Rafe's palm. "I will stay by your side, my lord, no matter your choices. I simply worry."

"I know. I appreciate your honesty." He kissed Kiran again and stepped away. "Now, get dressed and go feed yourself. I believe there's an eager young redhead who's taken a liking to you, isn't there?"

Kiran's lips twitched up into a smile. "Yes, there is."

AFTER KIRAN DRESSED and left, Rafe made his way down to the courtyard. The blacksmiths would be delivering his commission soon, and he wanted to see it safely stored until he and his contingent left the following morning.

Orienna, Rafe's second most loyal retainer after Kiran, stood on the top step of the staircase leading from the front of the manor to the courtyard. Her hair cascaded down her back in a sleek, straight tail, and he took a moment to appreciate the aesthetic. Black clothing fit close to her body from shoulder to knee, where tall boots began and outlined her calves. Only her arms were bare, as pale as Eamon's skin and starkly contrasted against the dark of her clothing. Rafe stopped beside her on the top step and clasped his hands behind him, mimicking her straight-backed posture. She was an imposing being, close to Rafe's height and built lean and graceful like a predator. If she weren't considerably younger than him and fiercely loyal, Rafe might have worried about a rivalry. She turned her head slightly to identify him and bowed at the waist. Rafe nodded in return, and she straightened.

"There is no way to know where you will find a ghoul or how long it will take," she said without preamble. "Are you sure it's wise to leave in such uncertainty?"

"I'm leaving the manor in your capable hands, Orienna. I am not worried. Most of the best soldiers and guards are still here to protect the village. Remember, I am to be contacted immediately in the event of a ghoul breach."

Orienna nodded, her long pale hair swishing side to side gently. "We will do our best to take it alive, my lord, or wait for you to arrive if you are near."

"Avoid casualties at all costs," he said, "but if the opportunity presents itself..."

She nodded. Her eyes had never stopped scanning the scene before them as they spoke, and Rafe took comfort in her behavior. She would be a good leader. Perhaps even better than him, if she had retainers as strong and loyal as she and Kiran were to him.

"Thank you, Orienna."

She finally turned her head to look at him more fully, and her thin lips curved into a smile. The expression melted her sharp features into something warm, and she took his hand, brought it to her lips, and kissed his knuckles.

"Anything I can do to be of service, my lord."

He smiled and kissed her forehead as he had Kiran's. She continued to smile, but her eyes lingered on him, and her sadness was obvious in the gaze. She, too, was afraid Rafe would not return from this adventure in one piece. That made three of them.

But he had to try.

Chapter Eleven

EAMON

Beah was not a talkative travelling companion, but Eamon didn't mind. The heat and terrain did nothing to make him chatty. They made it to the edge of the forest by nightfall, but he was too tired to enjoy it properly.

"It's too dangerous for a fire," Beah said, casting around for somewhere to bed down for the night. Eamon looked at him, wide-eyed.

"Does it get cold?"

"Not as cold as the desert."

"Are there...a lot of morroul?"

Beah nodded. "There are other creatures in the forest too. Some are afraid of fire. Others are attracted by it. The ones attracted are the most dangerous kind. It's not worth the risk."

"Gods above," Eamon muttered. Beah had stopped by a large fallen tree that created a small shelter and gestured to it with a questioning expression. Eamon shrugged. "I'm not going to sleep."

"You should."

"I won't be able to."

"Fine. Lay down and be quiet anyway."

Eamon unshouldered his pack and joined Beah in the shadow of the fallen tree. Though it was too dark to make out the finer details of the setting, the smell and texture of the air told Eamon they were in a healthy forest. It smelled green, the air cool and moist. In the morning, he'd be damp from sleeping in a bed of leaves and grass. Yes, this was familiar terrain, and though it probably had a hundred times more monsters, Eamon would take those risks over the risk of dying from sun poisoning. At least he could fight monsters. There was no fighting the sun.

They lay together, back to back under one blanket to share warmth. Though Eamon was tired, it took him a long time to fall asleep. Every cracking twig, creaking branch, or rustle of wind through the leaves made him fear for his life. He did his best to hold still so he wouldn't bother Beah, but the other man must surely feel his heart pounding through him where their backs touched. Beah didn't react, but he seemed too still and tense. Eamon didn't believe he was asleep.

Morning brought stiff muscles and a groggy head. He'd eventually fallen asleep, but strange dreams and discomfort had haunted him through the night. Beah would leave him today, and he'd be alone in this world and ill-prepared to face it.

They didn't speak as they took care of morning necessities. The only words spoken after they set off were Beah's soft, "This way. It's not far."

And it wasn't. They moved through knee-high vegetation for less than an hour before a familiar roaring sound reached Eamon. Rushing water. They kept walking until sloping muddy banks rolled down toward the river.

"This is it." Beah pointed upstream. "Follow this. In several days, you'll come to a white tree and a stream feeding into the river. Follow the stream. It will take you to the village. More or less."

Eamon's nerves were acting up again, filling him with a thousand "what if" scenarios, prime among them being what if he got lost? What if he wandered this forest until he died?

"I wish you'd come with me," he confessed, meeting Beah's eyes.

"Eamon—"

"I'm scared." There. He'd gotten the words out to a near-complete stranger, a kid no less. He'd often been told admitting the problem was the first step to solving it, but he needed help to solve this one.

They stood facing each other for a long time, the roar of the river drowning out all other sounds around them. Finally, Beah sighed and looked down.

"You recall I said my village worships the morroul?"

"Yes."

He paused, wiping a gloved hand against his leg. "Every season, we make offerings to the gods to thank them for our continued life and to entreat them to continue their protection and care for another season."

Offerings were common in religions, but with what little Beah had revealed about his past, Eamon didn't like where this new discussion was going.

"There is a lottery," Beah said. "This past season, I drew the lucky tile." He looked up and met Eamon's wide eyes. "I was sacrificed. I am meant to be dead, Eamon."

He stared at Beah for a moment, uncertain how to continue. Everyone joked about "virgin sacrifices" but no one had carried them out for hundreds of years. "W-what happened?"

Beah shook his head. "I panicked. They cut me and put me in the pit, and I tried to...to accept my fate. Put my life in the hands of the gods. But I couldn't. I think the lottery was fixed. It wasn't truly my fate, and I refused to accept it."

Eamon didn't know where to start with the questions. Cut him? Put him in a pit?

"Why would they fix the lottery to choose you?"

Beah shook his head, paused, and then said, "The priests called me 'troubled.' The girl who refused to dress like a girl, talk like a girl, wear her hair like a girl. They prayed for me, but I didn't change. So..." He shrugged. "The lottery was a convenient solution."

Eamon's brows went up. "They chose to *kill you* for being who you are?"

"For causing unrest." He looked down and shook his head again. "For being a troublemaker. A burden."

"You aren't a burden."

Beah stared at him with narrowed, thoughtful eyes and then said, "I wish more people thought like you, Eamon." He sighed. "Unfortunately, they don't. Most of the women my age were pregnant already, but I was the crazy girl running around with a sword, calling myself a man and refusing to marry. My mother was ashamed of me. My father is dead. My word didn't carry much weight. They were content to get rid of the problem, make it look like luck. If it's any consolation, they truly believe they were sending me to the gods."

Eamon kept his features under control and merely nodded, unsure of how to react. He'd grown up in a small village, and Seacliff was no grand metropolis, but he'd met enough people to know such identities weren't rare. The self-deprecating tone in Beah's words said he was used to being teased, disbelieved, and mistreated. Eamon knew enough to realize that wasn't rare either.

"I don't think you're crazy," Eamon said softly.

"Thank you." Beah looked down and away. They remained quietly by the riverbank for several moments before Beah spoke up. "You should be getting started, Eamon. It will take you at least seven days to reach the place where the stream leaves the mountains. The village is near there, but it's hidden. Look for an outcropping shaped like a boot. Even if you can't find it, the gatherers will find you."

The fear returned at the thought of leaving Beah. The distraction of conversation had calmed him, but now, at the thought of hiking for seven days through unfamiliar dangerous territory, looking for a white tree and an outcropping shaped like a boot?

He was going to die.

"You'll be fine," Beah said, reading the anxiety in his face. "You can hunt. The river is full of fish, and plenty of small animals live in the forest. You have an endless supply of water. Keep your cloak on if you're in direct sunlight." He smiled. "Tell the villagers you're looking for Alma. She's the only one who might be able to help. Do not mention..." He trailed off and shook his head. "They won't know me by this name. But do not mention me anyway. Ask for Alma."

"Who is she?"

"The priestess. She carries out the sacrifices. She's the one who might be able help you."

The words didn't reassure him, but he wasn't going to make a fool of himself sobbing and blubbering over his companion. Underneath everything, though, he was worried for his newfound savior.

"What about you?" he asked.

"What about me?"

"You're just going to live in a cave forever?"

"Not forever. Only until I decide on a way to prove I'm not insane."

"You would be welcome at Seacliff," he said again, in one last-ditch effort to draw Beah along with him.

"I wouldn't make it there. My return to the village would cause too much trouble."

Eamon wasn't certain *he* would make it there, either, but there was nothing left to do but try. With a deep breath, he squared his shoulders, lifted his chin, and said, "Thank you for everything, Beah. Please take care of yourself." Then he turned and followed the river.

Chapter Twelve

EAMON

If Eamon hadn't known he was in another world, he'd never have figured it out from the forest he now wandered through. Trees rose up around him, forming a green canopy that blotted out the two suns. The knee-high boots, which had been hot and uncomfortable in the desert, were now welcome protection against brambles and mud. He stayed within earshot of the river's roar, even when trees and foliage forced him away from the banks. It seemed impossible this side of the mountain range could be so lush when he'd come close to dying on the other side in the space of a couple days. Even the plants looked familiar. Eamon spotted berry vines laden with heavy black fruits that looked exactly like a plant back home. When he cautiously sampled one, he found it tasted familiar. Different than expected, but close enough. Gambling they weren't poisonous, he gathered a couple handfuls to snack on as he walked.

Travel between worlds had been much more common at one time, but King Soren closely monitored the little bit allowed these days. Eamon assumed it was monitored closely in the other worlds too—except this one, clearly. Unless there was some ghoul ruler who sent the ghouls through to his and Rafe's world.

Eamon slowed his pace, focusing on his thoughts. Did this world, or this specific division of it, have a ruler, like a king or lord? Were they ghoul, or human? If the humans of Beah's village regarded the ghouls as servants of the gods, he doubted the world's ruler would be human. Ghouls were a step above them in the celestial hierarchy. Were there rin here at all? If there were, surely they wouldn't let the ghouls run rampant. The two species were mortal enemies. If ghouls were the rulers here, this place must be an anarchy. Every village for itself.

He popped a berry in his mouth, cringed, and spat it aside. Not ripe.

Traveling alone had its perks. He set the pace. He didn't need to sneak into the bushes to relieve himself. If a plant or tree caught his interest, he investigated it at his leisure. When he got hungry, he ate, without regard for any etiquette—not that he had a lack of etiquette, after living in Rafe's manor for so long, and not as if there was much etiquette to be observed when dried meat and berries were the only food available. Traipsing through the forest with a pack on his back, stuffing his mouth full of berries plucked fresh from the vine, gave him distinct flashbacks to teenage years spent hiking and hunting with human friends, and, later, with Rafe.

When he first left home and moved to Seacliff village, it had been with his childhood friend—and at the time, lover—Tuomas at his side, one horse between them, and a caged falcon on their cart. They'd been young and brave and, in retrospect, pretty careless, but it'd been fun. Eamon was the one to suggest taking up a more permanent home in Seacliff after a temporary stay introduced him to a man named Bradley, the village falconry master. It didn't take long before Eamon's skill with his bird and his interest in the art convinced Bradley to take Eamon as an apprentice. Which was how he met Rafe.

It was clear to Eamon the rin who'd just walked in was not an average customer. The village had its share of rin, of course—Eamon had been getting better at picking them out in a crowd—but none of them wore silk or embroidery to the falcon house. And none of them came with an entourage. The tall rin had light brown skin, blue eyes, and long black hair hanging in a silky sheet around a sharp-featured face. His companions were on either end of the spectrum, one as pale as Eamon himself, and the other dark as midnight.

Bradley had gone to the herbalist for some supplies and left Eamon in charge. The rin stood with his hands clasped behind him, looking around the large open building with a curious expression. It was similar to a stable, but instead of horse stalls, cages lined both side walls and the back wall, leaving the front open for customers to enter and stand. Eamon approached the visitors and offered a half bow.

"How may I help you, my lord?"

The rin looked at him, did a double take, and stared for several seconds—for so long it made Eamon uneasy. He'd dealt with rin before and didn't share his family's beliefs about them, but he was acutely aware they fed on humans, and he didn't stand a chance of defending himself against one. The villagers had kind things to say about their Lord Rafe, but what if this wasn't him?

"What is your name?" the rin asked, finally, his voice low. It had a musical lilt, taking away some of what Eamon might have found threatening in such a voice otherwise.

"Eamon, my lord."

"Eamon." He nodded. "I am Rafe."

Relieved, Eamon took a deep breath and let it out slowly. Rafe's lips quirked to the side in an expression barely resembling a smile, but it seemed to imply amusement.

"You were more afraid I was not the Lord than you are to find out I am?"

"I've heard good things about you, my lord. It's an honor to meet you." Eamon bowed again, deeper that time. "I was afraid if you were not...you...then you were someone I knew nothing about."

Rafe's quirky little smile widened, and he leaned on one of the wide posts with his shoulder, hands casually slipped into his pockets. His companions stayed near the door. Eamon hadn't noticed how far into the room Rafe had come until he realized how far away his two companions stood. For all intents and purposes, Rafe and Eamon were alone with the birds.

"Well, Eamon, I am glad you've heard good things about me, but I have heard nothing about you. I was told Bradley had taken on an apprentice. I've been remiss not to come meet you. I apologize."

Eamon smiled. "I would not expect you to come meet me, Lord Rafe. I'm just an apprentice falconer."

"Just an apprentice," Rafe echoed, tilting his head thoughtfully. He pushed away from the support he'd been leaning on and began to walk along the row of cages against the wall, inspecting falcons and hawks and eagles with a critical eye. He moved with the eerie grace most older rin possessed. It was what set them apart from humans—young rin were virtually indistinguishable from humans, but the older they got,

the less human-like they became. It was in their gait, their posture, their eyes. Rafe had the elegance of a cat, and, until that moment, Eamon had never in his life so desired to be a mouse.

He tried to ignore the sudden lust and focus on his customer's needs.

"W-what can I help you with today, my lord?"

"To be honest, I'm bored." Rafe paused by a large golden eagle. He looked up into its cage, and the bird seemed to meet his eyes. Eamon wondered what two perfect predators would see in each other. Would they see the other as challenge, or comrade?

"Bored?" Eamon repeated. Ugh, clever. Rafe kept walking, and Eamon had to turn to track his progress along the wall. "Do you have a falcon already, my lord?"

"No. I'm interested in learning the art." He glanced over his shoulder at Eamon. "How long have you been practicing, Eamon?"

"Since childhood, my lord."

"So, if I need advice, you are qualified to provide it?" Rafe hadn't stopped walking, now prowling along the back wall. Eamon turned to keep him in his sight, getting the distinct impression he was more interesting to Rafe than the birds were.

"I am, my lord," he said, "but if I may be so bold, a bird isn't a simple amusement to cure boredom. They're intelligent animals and deserve the best care and attention."

Rafe broke away from the perimeter and crossed to Eamon, who took a couple nervous steps back before catching himself and forcing his feet to hold still. He let Rafe approach, nervous excitement fluttering in his chest and...elsewhere. Gods, Tuomas would laugh at him, getting so aroused from a simple conversation while surrounded by the musty barn smell of the falcon house. The rin stopped an arm's length away. A safe distance for them both.

"I do not take anything lightly, Eamon. I do not invest myself in a venture unless I am fully committed to it. I do not play around."

"O-of course, Lord Rafe," Eamon managed.

And then Rafe smiled properly for the first time, and Eamon's breath stuck in his throat. Gods, he was stunning. "Would you be interested in teaching me the art, or should I make a request directly to Master Bradley?"

"I can teach you," Eamon said, perhaps too eagerly. He had confidence in his falconry skills. He didn't have confidence he wouldn't strip naked and beg Rafe to have his body right here and now if the rin didn't stop looking at him like that though. As if detecting Eamon's imminent disrobing, Rafe nodded and turned his attention to the birds.

"Do I choose the bird, or does the bird choose me?"

Eamon took a deep breath and let it out slowly. "I believe it has to be a mutual choice, my lord."

Rafe glanced at him and smiled again. "I am open-minded. I respect those who respect me. I have high standards, but I am not unreasonable. Do you know any who would choose me based on those traits?"

Me, Eamon thought, and from Rafe's expression, he got the strangest sensation the rin lord knew exactly what he wanted to say. He forced himself to focus again and began asking the standard expected questions of curious new falconers, to help them choose a bird to meet their needs and mesh with their temperament.

In the end, Rafe selected a beautiful red-tailed hawk. As he paid Eamon for the bird, cage, and equipment, he smiled again.

"It has been an honor to watch you work today, Eamon. Would you like to have dinner with me tonight? We can discuss your available times for teaching me to hunt."

Eamon had never been invited to dinner by a rin. Did "dinner" secretly mean Rafe wanted to feed from him? If he agreed to come to dinner, was he giving consent to be fed on? Seeing his hesitation—and correctly guessing its cause—Rafe clarified with a gentle smile.

"Food. We will both eat food. I am not asking to draw from your vein or taste your life."

"Oh," Eamon breathed. "Then yes, my lord. I would love to have dinner with you tonight."

"Be at the gate before sunset. The guards will be waiting for you."

Eamon bowed, heart racing. He trembled like a nervous fool for the rest of the afternoon.

Chapter Thirteen

EAMON

Fond memories kept Eamon company through the first day and into the second. The night was restful only because he was so tired from walking that his fatigued body overrode his anxious mind. At home, he tended to lay awake half the night caught up in thoughts. Maybe once he returned to Seacliff, he'd convince Rafe to help him reach a point of complete physical exhaustion every night so he was actually able to sleep. The thought made him grin.

He'd spotted a few forest critters and dozens of birds as he hiked, but by nightfall on the second day, one thing he hadn't seen was a ghoul. In fact, he'd forgotten to be on the lookout for them. Everything was so peaceful in the forest. It was the place Eamon was most at ease. His fear at being left alone to find Beah's village had ebbed when hungry ghouls or bears or other monsters hadn't immediately descended on him, and he was able to find peace as he walked. Birds flitted from branch to branch, chirping without a care in the world. The river's gurgling roar lulled him into a meditation, and he managed to convince himself he was in the forest outside Seacliff village, flying his falcon or letting one of the stray village dogs keep him company. And when he got tired, he'd just find the path and head home, crawl into bed with Rafe and have amazing sex and fall asleep in his arms.

The illusion was shattered when a branch cracked somewhere nearby, and all of Eamon's nerves exploded into overdrive. He'd moved into a thicket to sleep, away from the bare banks of the river, hoping it would be less likely for anything stalking in the darkness to spot him. Now, he wondered if sleeping on the bank so *he* could see things stalking him wouldn't have been a better idea. He'd slept alone in the forest before, but never one with monsters taller than two people put together.

And, judging by the way his heart was pounding, he wouldn't be sleeping, alone or otherwise, in this forest that night. He tried to get comfortable and control his breathing, but another branch snapped, and he shoved aside the blanket and grabbed his bow and quiver. Without a fire to see by and the light of the moon barely shining through the branches, he'd have to rely on his other senses. The night birds had gone silent. No yips or growls or barks came from nocturnal dogs, no snorts or scuffs from deer or boar. The river rushed along its course, flowing out into eternity, and the soft rustle of leaves in a gust of wind—no... The soft rustle of leaves against *flesh*. The soft gust of *breath* from huge lungs.

Eamon stopped breathing. It was close. It was snuffling like an animal on a scent, coming upstream.

Gods. It was tracking him. It was tracking him; it was *tracking him*. His heart had to be pounding loud enough for the thing to hear it. He fought for calm, for the quiet focus of a hunt, the attention to detail that allowed him to drive arrows directly into the eyes of his prey.

Except he wasn't hunting. He had no prey. This beast was hunting *him*.

He peered around the broad tree trunk he was pressed against and tried to make out a shape.

Within range of his arrows, a hulking shadow blocked the cool light of the moon reflecting off the river. Quietly, Eamon drew one arrow from the quiver at his hip and lay it against the bow, breathing deeply. His back and legs ached from tension, his body tight as the bowstring against his fingers, ready to break at the slightest nick of a blade. Or claws.

Perhaps if he held very still, it would pass him up. It would catch the scent of a boar or something meatier. It would...it would...

Gods. *Gods*, please, he hadn't come this far just to die in the dark, alone. Please. He wanted to make it home, he wanted Rafe, he wanted to live the rest of his life out with his lover and make love and read books together and go hunting together until they were both too old to ride a horse anymore and their eyes went bad and they had to hire someone to read books to them while they lay in each other's arms, he did not want *this*, he was not going to die like *this*!

There. Anger. Righteous indignation and fury. It overrode the fear like a stampede of horses, like a tidal wave crashing over the panic and shattering it across the sand.

He leaned around the tree trunk again, and this time, he watched the shadow long enough to determine its shape and find its head. It was hunchbacked and human-like, with huge thick forearms and a small head perched atop broad, muscular shoulders. It resembled a giant hellacious version of the tree-dwelling monkeys inhabiting the forest around his childhood home.

It lifted its head. In his mind, Eamon saw the thing catching his scent, focusing in on him with beady black eyes. He couldn't be sure where those beady black eyes were, but he had a clear line of sight to the monster, so he did his best to guess, trained his arrow, and let fly.

The creature let out a shriek of fury and pain, sending roosting birds fleeing into the night. Eamon resisted the urge to flee as well—until the creature did not fall, but, instead, turned its considerable bulk toward him and began running. It shouldered saplings aside like irritating children in the market square, and Eamon had time to nock and release two more arrows before he made the decision to run. The darkness, so peaceful only moments ago, shattered with the cacophony of a slaughterhouse now, full of braying, and pained and angry screams.

Bending, Eamon snatched his bag from the ground and bolted into the forest in the general direction he'd come from. He knew better than to run directly away from a charging predator and tried to confuse it by bolting past it, hoping in its rage and pain it would not have enough reason to turn and follow.

For a few strides, he thought he'd succeeded. The resounding *crack!* that came from his chosen sleeping place made him think the ghoul had attacked the tree. Eamon wasn't sure if the tree won, or the ghoul.

Then, another crack, and another, interspersed with the enraged screams of a creature in agony. Was it attacking the tree? Did it think the tree had shot arrows at it? Ghouls didn't seem to be very bright.

A familiar series of cracks and strained groans made Eamon pick up his feet again. He hadn't meant to stop running, but it had seemed his plan was working. Now, the creature's rage was about to send a tree toppling to the ground, and Eamon wasn't certain he was far enough away to avoid the fallout. He started running again, heedless of the noise he was making.

The ghoul roared and then began smashing through the trees behind him.

Fuck! Eamon risked a glance over his shoulder, but it was too dark to make out any more than a blob of mobile darkness moving inside the overall darkness of the forest. The blob was moving fast, though, and it was large, and he didn't think he was going to outrun it. Behind and above them both, the crashing of branches against branches grew louder.

Eamon screamed. The ghoul roared. Something struck him hard in the back, bearing him to the ground, claws and teeth raking at his ill-protected flesh, and he shrieked until his lungs burned, too surprised and pained to worry about attracting attention. He was going to die now, here in the forest, alone, under the hungry mouth of a flesh-eating monster.

He blacked out.

Chapter Fourteen

RAFE

Kiran rode at his side without a word for the entire first day. Rafe had brought a small contingent of soldiers to travel with him, as well as a few humans to keep his rin alive, bringing the group to nine members including himself.

To the south of them lay an area known for rampant ghoul breaches. Rafe wasn't clear on how travel between worlds worked, but there had to be some kind of process allowing targeted entry, or gatekeepers wouldn't be as useful as King Soren found them. Why the ghouls targeted this specific area, he had no idea, but most of the ones turning up at Seacliff Manor were likely strays that had broken through in this breach zone and come north. If they were going to find a ghoul to interrogate or manipulate, Rafe guessed it would be the best place to start.

At nightfall, they stopped at a village and rented all the empty rooms at the inn. Rafe didn't care about drawing attention, even with all the curiosity surrounding his recent behavior. His lands stretched far, and he made an effort to visit every village at least once a year. But it wouldn't hurt his image to visit more often. Though he had a reputation of being strict, he was well liked.

Kiran came to Rafe's bed after he'd fed himself. He disrobed and slipped under the blankets at Rafe's side without a word.

"You must be hungry," he murmured.

Rafe rolled toward him and lay a palm on his chest, and their eyes met. Kiran gasped as the connection was forged, then moaned as he allowed his mind to be entered and Rafe flooded it with pleasure. The blanket tented up at Kiran's loins, and Rafe smiled and pulled it aside to expose his servant. Kiran's hands were fisted in the sheet; Rafe pulled one loose and moved it to Kiran's cock. The rin got the hint and began stroking himself.

With Eamon, Rafe would take his time. He wouldn't artificially inflate the sensations, unless Eamon asked him to. He would kiss and touch, suck and nip and stroke and pet. Eamon would beg, spread his legs, rut up into the air with pleas falling from his lips like water from a pitcher.

Rafe wondered if Kiran would be so wanton. Most likely. Even during this small act, his retainer's desire washed over him, his delight at being driven to such pleasure by his lord and master. As Kiran stroked himself, Rafe opened himself up to receive Kiran's life energy. It floated off Kiran in smoky wisps as the pleasure built.

He pushed Kiran's mind to perceive pleasure more strongly and petted his chest. Such a little bit of contact, but it was all Kiran needed—his fist jerked faster, and he whimpered between each gasped breath. As orgasm approached, more of his defenses fell, and Rafe drew more from him, pulling in the energy creeping out through lowered guards. The instant orgasm hit, everything still protecting Kiran's energy, whether intentional or not, shattered, and Rafe took in a great breath, absorbing what Kiran could spare. As long as Rafe continued to touch Kiran, drawing in his life, Kiran shuddered head to toe, struck with wave after wave of pleasure. Rafe's body responded to his partner's orgasm and to the influx of energy, and he grew hard against the bed. It would be easy to keep Kiran riding the wave and to keep taking life from him until his heart gave out, no longer able to sustain the physical demands of orgasm without the life energy to maintain a heartbeat.

In some parts of the world, humans did not allow themselves to be fed on. Hundreds of years ago, young rin frequently killed their human prey by taking too much from them. In pursuit of harmony between the species, more strict measures had been enforced to keep humans from turning into casualties every time a rin hungered. In some places, Rafe's relationship with Eamon would be seen as disgusting or manipulative, parasitic even. It was difficult to find common ground with people who found one's very existence sickening.

Rafe lifted his hand off Kiran's chest and watched as his companion went limp and shivered through aftershocks. He smiled. Kiran looked up at him and smiled too, dizzy and drunk with pleasure.

"I wish I could do the same for you," he whispered.

Rafe shook his head and smiled. "You do enough, Kiran." He rolled onto his back and stared up at the ceiling. "You do enough."

IT WAS THE third day of travel when they came across something worth notice. Kourt—a skilled tracker—held up her hand, reined in, and dismounted. She walked to the edge of the road, slowly, then, in the blink of an eye, went down the brief incline and disappeared into the forest.

Sier, Kourt's mate, swore. "She found something."

Rafe was already on the ground and following before Sier finished his words.

The rin swore again and dismounted to follow, the rest of the contingent on their heels. But before long, Rafe didn't need Kourt's tracking skills to find the ghoul. A gentle breeze carried the creature's stench.

They came into a small clearing. Just ahead, a fruit orchard rose up the gentle swell of a hill. Branches swayed as something large moved through the trees.

"Remember," Rafe said as his soldiers formed up around him, "we are disabling it, not killing it."

"Yes, my lord."

They were skeptical, but he'd asked for volunteers for this endeavor. Everyone was here because they wanted to be, because they wanted to help him. Rafe had to admit he was a little skeptical himself. He wasn't certain if ghouls were able to speak—but it didn't matter either way. The part of the plan he hadn't bothered to tell anyone about meant speech wasn't actually required.

Half the group went around the rustling trees and flushed the thing out into the clearing, toward where Rafe, Kiran, and two others waited.

This ghoul was a hellacious thing with long, spindly limbs, a thin body, and rubbery flesh the color of the darkest night. Its head seemed too large by comparison, spherical and full of teeth barely fitting its wide gash of a mouth. Rafe knew immediately the shackles he'd had commissioned would not hold such small wrists. The monster was twice as tall as a human, but its wrists were probably no thicker around. Perhaps he would just chop its limbs off altogether. Dismemberment would be more effective than shackles, and probably more satisfying.

And then he had no more time to think about it. The thing was upon him and his group, and it immediately sent one of his soldiers sailing across the clearing to crash into a tree with a sickening *thwump*. Thin, maybe, but not frail. Rafe threw himself at it with all the pent-up rage he'd been holding inside for over a week.

The ghoul moved like lightning to dodge Rafe's first strike. It did a backward flip over Sier's head, grabbed him from behind, and tore at his throat with its long claws. Kourt shrieked as her bound mate's blood shot across the grass, and she fell to her knees. A sharp pang of pain in his chest, and Rafe knew his soldier was dead. He spun to Kiran.

"Get them out of here!"

Before Kiran had time to move, Kourt threw herself at the ghoul with a primal scream of fury, slashing at its scrawny limbs. It seemed capable of bending them in every direction. She got in a solid slash across its back as it flipped away. The thing let out its own shriek of anger and closed on her. Rafe lunged at its side, but it bore Kourt to the ground before he was able to get to it, and she was gone in seconds.

Her blood splashed across the ghoul's arms, and it froze. The creature hunched over her, and Rafe realized as he swung it was entranced by her scent. Her human blood.

"Filth!" he screamed and tackled the monster. Rafe was no larger than a human, but he had the strength of two hundred years behind him and was able to knock it off of her. They rolled. Someone screamed Rafe's name. He lost his sword in the scuffle, but before the ghoul did to him what it had done to Sier and Kourt, he grabbed its head and made eye contact—and dove.

It didn't matter if the ghoul was able to speak. He didn't need to speak its language to read its mind.

Somewhere outside his thoughts, people were screaming.

"Rafe!"

"My lord!"

"No, wait!"

Even as he plunged into the ghoul's mind, he recognized the last voice as Kiran's. Then he had to shut it all out and focus to keep the thing sedated.

Rafe had suspected it was possible to get in a ghoul's head. It was easy to get into animals' minds, and he could do all kinds of things to humans and other rin. There was no way a ghoul would be more difficult than any of those.

And he was right. It wasn't. Inside its mind, he felt *hunger. Anger. Lust.* He expected all those—the mind of a stray dog was not much different—but the power of them was enough to make him want to pull away, to retreat from the predatory mind for fear of losing himself to the torrent of primal needs.

No. Eamon. Find Eamon.

The hunger pulled at him the worst. It was a sensation he was familiar with—as a being that fed on other living things, there was a fine line between satisfying those needs without violating trust or endangering lives. As a young rin, the craving for life became so strong he thought he might drown in it at times. Things had not been as easy in his youth, but he'd never been willing to take without consent. He'd learned to fight it.

Which meant he had ways to fight the ghoul's hunger too. The needs and sensations flowed around him, pulsing with the ghoul's thundering heartbeat, threatening to overwhelm him. He concentrated on himself, his mind, the conscious thoughts formed between his needs and the outside world, between this ghoul's needs and himself. The thoughts kept him stiff-backed, chin up, and posture perfect when he stood before his people. He was a leader, a lord, not some common animal to allow his basest needs to overwhelm his civility. He was a caretaker, a master, and a lover. He had Eamon. He had to find Eamon.

Clinging to his own personality, Rafe pushed past the hunger and desires of the beast and sought out something more complex. There had to be some sense of reason. He moved for its memories, casting over the sea of its mind like a scryer searching for clues.

Where had it come from?

There. *Desert. Orange stone surrounded by orange sky. A river in a canyon. Two suns. Little food. Hunger.*

How did it get here?

Hungry. Smelled blood. Followed.

Rafe sank into the memory, tripping into it like he'd stepped off the last stair in the staircase, only to realize it *wasn't* the last, and he was falling, heart in his throat.

He was alone. He'd left the forest behind days ago and now wandered through a field of tall grass at the base of a red-orange mountain.

The creature's actions were as familiar to Rafe as if they'd been his own. Its spindly body moved with a strange, uneven gait somewhere between jumping and crawling. The tall grass brushed against its bare limbs as it trundled through the field. Moonlight cast eerie shadows around it as grass rustled and waved in the breeze.

There was a place near here. It smelled of food there. Blood.

From the thing's mind, Rafe knew approximately how far the "place" was, and its ability to smell blood from such a distance gave him chills. This thing was the perfect predator, evolved for the single purpose of killing and eating. In a place as inhospitable as its world, it only made sense for the dominant life to be well developed for survival. And it didn't surprise him either, that humans could survive in such a place. If there was any life-form more adaptable and capable of survival in inhospitable climates than humans, he hadn't yet discovered it.

The place was near. The smell of blood stronger now. The hunger ached in his belly.

A large rock shifted in the distance. No, not a rock. An enemy. Competition. He sped up. It stood from the grass, and he saw it was smaller than him. Barely even worth notice. He bypassed it and kept running. The grass was thinning out as he approached the very base of the mountains. The smaller ghoul was unable to keep pace with him.

Almost there. Blood. Hunger. Pain. A sound— screaming. The screaming of prey.

Another ghoul seemed to materialize from nowhere and approach from the other side. So focused on the smell of blood, he hadn't noticed the creature until it was nearly on top of him, but it didn't come for him. It was going for the blood and the shrieks of fear too.

Rafe tried to look around in the ghoul's memory, to take in the surroundings better, but it was so single-minded on food, it hadn't noticed anything. The setting was familiar to it; it had been here before, but then, too, it hadn't paid much heed to the scenery. The grasslands ended at orange-brown mountains, and Rafe was unable to determine more. Giving up on the landscape, he returned to the ghoul's memory, though he had a sickening feeling he didn't want to know what happened next.

He arrived at a hole in the ground, deep enough a human wouldn't be able to jump and reach the top edge. The source of the smell and the sound. He stepped up to the edge and curled his long, bony fingers into the soil, gripping as he peered down. The setting sun left the bottom of the pit dark, but a small shape huddled in the shadows reeked of fear, blood, tears, and pain. Delicious. He began crawling down into the pit. The other ghoul, the one he hadn't noticed approaching, was not so slow about its descent and merely dove in after its prey. Rage erupted in his mind, and he let loose from the wall and dropped onto the other ghoul's furred back, shoving all his claws into the soft tissue of its flanks like daggers. It let out a shriek. The human prey let out a shriek.

The human was small, brown-skinned and dark-haired. A child? The pit was too strange to be anything but man-made. He couldn't think of a reason why a squarish pit would be open in the middle of a field. From the ghoul's memories and knowledge, Rafe guessed this was a place where humans, bleeding and afraid, often "appeared." The ghoul hadn't much in the way of reasoning skills to determine how or why or even be curious about such things, but Rafe did, and he was, and he felt sick with the possibilities. There had to be a settlement nearby. Lone people didn't wander into a field and jump into a pit to be eaten by ghouls of their own accord. Were they criminals? Was this punishment? Surely not, if the person in the pit was a child.

He was fighting, slamming the other ghoul into the wall. Soil rained down on their bodies. Over the fury and pain, he barely registered another voice, this one not scared. It was a woman speaking calmly from above, and suddenly, he was falling through a blinding light.

When he hit the ground, it wasn't the same ground he'd known before. The smells weren't the same. The sounds weren't the same. The sky wasn't the same.

That was enough. This ghoul hadn't come to Rafe's world under its own power. A human had sent it. Why? How? Rafe pawed through the thing's memories, but all he got was eating and fighting and hunting. Nothing to help him find Eamon.

Rafe gathered himself and drew away from the creature's mind. As he did, he became aware of his physical surroundings, the tension of his companions, and snappish voices.

At the instant he withdrew from the ghoul's mind, its body thrashed. Whenever he left Eamon's mind, or Kiran's, their reaction was usually dizziness. The ghoul's reaction was blind fury. It let out a feral roar. Rafe was fast, but in its rage, the ghoul wasn't concerned with self-preservation. Its claws came directly to its own chest, intent on grabbing the annoyance daring to invade its mind. Rafe rolled to the side, but a claw managed to catch his left leg. He screamed as it raked through his flesh like a knife through soft fruit.

His companions piled onto the thing at once. Rafe had the presence of mind to scramble out of their way, moving like a crab, dragging his injured leg. Rin were exceptionally resilient to infection and illness and healed more quickly than humans, but blood loss would prove deadly if the wound was severe. The dagger-like claw had gone deep, and Rafe's trouser leg was soaked. Pain interfered with focus and his hands shook as he gripped the fabric to tear it open further. His roll had allowed the claw to curve around his leg, starting near his hip and ending behind his knee where the thick leather of his boot had slowed it.

A roar of agony drew Rafe's fleeting focus up, and he saw the creature collapse, spurting black blood from its throat. It had barely hit the ground before Kiran was at Rafe's side, sword discarded.

"My lord." He was removing his belt. Rafe mustered a smile.

"Kiran, this is not an appropriate place to undress."

"This is not an appropriate place to die either, my lord," he said, moving quickly to wrap his belt around Rafe's leg. "You're a damn fool, you know."

Rafe groaned and lay back on the ground, nodding. "I know."

"I'm still not going to let you die though."

"I appreciate it, Kiran." He managed another smile, but he'd lost all sensation in his leg—not a good sign. And the worst part was he hadn't learned anything useful. This ghoul, at least, had been thrown into his world. They would have to find another, and another, until they found one with the ability to tear the veil.

First, he would have to stop bleeding out all over the forest floor.

Chapter Fifteen

BEAH

Beah tried to ignore the guilt and shame as he watched Eamon disappear into the trees. He told himself it was for the best—he had no business returning to his village, especially with everything he'd done since he left. He'd always wondered about following a god who demanded they feed someone to giant monsters every season. Since he'd seen what Alma did to those sacrifices, and to the morroul meant to feed on them...and since he'd eaten morroul and knew for certain they weren't messengers from the gods, he didn't think he would be able to return home even if his own mother appeared before him and begged. And he'd have no business going to Eamon's home, even if things worked out to make it an option. Live by the sea, in a forest on a cliff? It sounded like a child's story. He doubted anything would truly be different there.

No, he had to find his own way. He'd tried to do things their way. He'd tried to play a demure village woman, hoping the *wrongness* of it might fade in time as he aged, as his current life grew more important and his past life faded from his mind, but no. The feeling had never faded. All he'd had in the village was a miserable lie, a shadow of a true life. Out here, there'd be no one to call him "girl," or comment or judge or fight with him for trying to bind his chest. No one to tell him he was *pretty,* and he could keep his smooth cheeks hidden as much as he wanted without repercussion.

Yet...he was lonely. After so long alone, he'd welcomed Eamon's voice and his company. The fear when he saw how unwell Eamon had been, the relief when the man had woken and begun recovering... It had filled him with joy and pride—feelings he'd sorely missed since leaving home. As much as he hated being forced into womanly roles, he'd never resented learning cures and treatments. He enjoyed helping others, having contact and communication with other people. He just preferred to have such contact on his own terms, not some elder's, or his mother's, or anyone else who wanted to force him into things. And Eamon had never said a word about his identity. He'd never questioned it. He'd never even looked *confused* about it, even when Beah had intentionally "slipped up" and labeled himself a girl.

And Beah had just left him alone in an unfamiliar forest full of ghouls after essentially saying "not my problem." After Eamon offered him a new place to live, a place among people who wouldn't question or judge.

A place where creatures called "rin" lived. Eamon had told him about his lover, Rafe, and the bond they shared. He'd told him how these rin fed, through blood or sex, but never harmed their human victims, and only took with consent. That sounded like a children's story too. And perhaps Eamon was just saying things to avoid being left alone in the forest.

The gods have a plan for us all, his father used to say. *But sometimes, those plans are to let us make our own plans.* His father wouldn't have forced him to be a woman. But his father was dead.

Night was falling by the time Beah made it back to the small cave, but by the time he got there, he'd reached a decision. The gods hadn't struck him down for leaving the village, as he'd been told his whole life they would do. He doubted they would strike him down for leaving the world. Hiding in a cave was no less a shadow of a life than hiding in a village. Not when Eamon's world held promise of something so much better.

He gathered the few belongings he'd left in his temporary home, threw them in his bag, and went to the pool nearby to refill his waterskins. Eamon had a day of travel under his belt already. By the time Beah made it to the forest again, Eamon would have two days on him.

He threw his pack over his shoulder and headed the way he'd come, into the darkness. The terrain was familiar enough by now he was able to traverse some distance at night. Eamon would have the sense not to move at night. This was the only way Beah would catch up.

BEAH TRAVELED HALF the night before fatigue slowed him, and he bedded down under an outcrop of stone. In the morning, he ate as he walked, trying to save time and hoping Eamon didn't do the same. The man was eager to return to his lover, though, so Beah couldn't count on him taking his time or even being logical. Love had a way of clouding the mind he'd never quite understood.

If he made better time than Eamon, perhaps he'd be able to catch up by nightfall or shortly after. Assuming Eamon slept through the night while Beah walked, he'd cut half a day off the other's two-day lead.

He alternated between a fast walk and an easy jog, trotting down hills as quickly as possible without slipping in scree. The last thing he needed was to fall and break his neck—or worse, break a leg and die slowly of starvation.

Gods. What was he thinking? He'd all but given up on Shadelin, the god of this world—none of his prayers were ever answered, none of his offerings ever accepted, and he'd never received any signs or visions from the heavens like others in his village—but he sent up a prayer as he walked.

"I'm making my own plan, Shadelin. You're probably not listening, but if you are, I just ask that you let me go." He walked a few more steps, breathing hard, then said, "If you give a shit about me, let me know. This is your last chance with me."

Nothing happened, and Beah shook his head. Gods or no gods, he was done with the place.

He came to the edge of the forest and set out for the river.

Eamon said he'd been raised in the forest, and Beah soon realized it meant he'd be adept at not leaving signs of his passing. Either he was being sneaky, or he'd chosen to move far from the river's banks. Either way, Beah wasn't able to pick up his trail. He didn't have much tracking experience anyway. He'd never been included in hunting parties even when he asked to be.

He didn't waste much time trying to find Eamon's exact trail. He just set off in the direction he'd sent Eamon, the direction his pale companion had headed when they parted ways. He was making good time, eating while he walked, only taking breaks when absolutely necessary, but night still found him before he found Eamon. He didn't dare travel through the forest in the dark.

Tucked under a bush on the verge of sleep, Beah's entire body jerked to attention at a familiar, unwanted sound: a morroul roar. It turned his blood cold and set his body into a sweat; bumps pricked up over his skin and he trembled like a frightened rodent.

The instantaneous bone-deep fear was followed by fear of a different kind when the thing roared again. *Eamon!*

He was blind in the forest. He had no light. Fire was dangerous—it would attract morroul.

It would attract morroul...

With a heaving chest and shaky hands, Beah groped through his bag. He found the few items he hadn't had to use in weeks and went to work. Moments later, he had a makeshift torch from a strip of oil-soaked fabric wrapped around a branch. He made sure he had his sword, took a deep breath, and headed toward the furious cacophony.

He'd barely gone two steps when a distinctly human scream joined the roaring, crashing madness.

"Eamon!"

The torch cast a flickering orange light over bushes and undergrowth, lengthening branches and deepening ruts. Even with its light, he should move carefully...but he was too worried to be careful. A huge, resounding crash followed the screams, and then everything fell silent. Beah stopped, holding the torch above his head, shaking.

"Eamon?"

If the ghoul had survived, shouting and waving a torch was no way to go about surviving.

If Eamon had survived, shouting and waving a torch might be the only way for *him* to survive.

If Eamon was dead, well...perhaps Beah's foolish screaming and torch waving would attract the "sign" he'd asked for earlier in his prayer.

When nothing immediately leapt on him from the shadows or answered his call, he continued moving, torch raised high, calling out occasionally. His heart skipped a beat when a startled voice answered him.

"Beah?"

"Eamon?" He spun toward the voice, brandishing his torch. Light flashed over a ghastly white shape—a pale human face. Eamon lay in the underbrush, half-hidden under brambles and branches. "Are you hurt?"

"There's a ghoul," Eamon said, twisting to look over his shoulder. "There was, anyway...I don't know...I thought it..."

He was incomprehensible. Beah nodded and spoke slowly, holding the torch aside to avoid blinding his friend.

"Let's get you out of there. Are you hurt?"

Eamon's response came in his native language, and then, belatedly, he spoke in their shared tongue. "Are you real?"

"I'm real."

"Are you sure?"

Beah smiled. "I'm sure."

"You told me it was too dangerous for fire. What're you doing?"

"Looking for you," Beah said, pulling in every ounce of patience and calm he had left. "Eamon, *are you hurt*?"

The other man grunted and shook his head slowly. "Dunno. Yeah. Maybe. Hit my head. I think I pissed myself."

"Oh," Beah said, cheeks warming in embarrassment even as his shoulders slouched in relief. Eamon seemed unharmed, just a little dazed. "Well...we can take care of that. Come on. We need to get out of here before things come to see what happened here."

He kept the torch in his left hand and turned, offering his right to Eamon. It took some maneuvering, but they managed to get Eamon out from under the tangle of branches. As soon as he was free, he rolled onto his side and groaned, but Beah grabbed his arm and pulled.

"Get up."

"The world is spinning."

"I can't carry you, Eamon. Get up."

Somewhere not far away, something roared. Eamon lunged to his feet in fear—then swayed, staggered, and dropped to his knees, vomiting in the undergrowth. Beah cringed. There was nothing to be done about him vomiting and pissing and probably bleeding all over the place. Any other ghouls coming here to see what had happened would smell him. Beah hoped they didn't follow their scent.

With an arm around Eamon's waist, Beah managed to get them from the fallen tree to where he'd originally set up his camp. Eamon didn't speak, and moved with more certainty as the walk progressed, but Beah still worried. He'd seen awful things happen to people after hitting their heads.

"You shouldn't sleep," he said as he lowered Eamon to the ground and propped him up against the trunk of a tree.

"What?"

"When you hit your head hard enough to be disoriented, sleep can make things worse. You need to stay awake."

Again, somewhere too close for comfort, a creature made a horrible noise, and Eamon shifted to look toward it, but there was only darkness. Beah extinguished the torch with a bit of dirt and water.

"I don't think I'd sleep if I tried," Eamon said. Beah sat beside him, his own back against the trunk, their shoulders pressed together. "Are we safe?"

"No," Beah said.

Eamon snorted. "No comforting lies from you."

Beah glanced at him. The moonlight filtering through tree branches reflected on Eamon's skin, giving him an eerie glow. Ghouls weren't visual hunters, as far as Beah knew, and he was glad. Eamon was like a beacon in the darkness.

"Thank you," Eamon said after a moment. His hand left his lap and came over to Beah's lap, seeking his hand to give it a squeeze. "Thank you for coming after me."

"I apologize for ever leaving." Beah returned the squeeze and let go. "Are you hurt other than hitting your head?"

"No," Eamon said. "Nothing major. Sore. Tender. Nothing broken, I think."

"Good."

"What am I supposed to do all night if I can't sleep? Sit here?"

Beah looked up to the canopy, the vague suggestion of light above the trees. "Tell me more about your world."

His companion hummed. "It's a large world. I can't tell you everything about it."

"Tell me about your home, then."

"Seacliff?"

"If that's where you live, yes."

Eamon hummed again. His head lolled to the side a little, and Beah nudged him with his elbow.

"I'm awake, I'm awake..."

"Seacliff," Beah prompted.

"Right. Um...I moved there not long after I reached adulthood. Probably around your age. My friend, Tuomas, went with me. We wanted to get a clean start away from our parents."

"I understand the feeling," Beah said.

"We grew up in a tiny village with very religious parents," Eamon said. His words were interrupted by a yawn, and Beah nudged his shoulder.

"Stay awake."

"I'm trying."

"Your parents?"

"Oh. Yeah. It's been a hundred years since humans and rin integrated worldwide, but some places still don't accept it. My parents didn't. Said it was unnatural and interfered with the gods' plans for us. I didn't agree. So I left."

"To find a rin to...integrate with?"

Eamon chuckled. "No. Well, I wasn't opposed to the idea, but mostly I didn't like being around closed minds. I wanted to see the world. You know how it is."

"Yes." Even though the preachers in his community forbade leaving the hidden village, swore up and down it was far too dangerous in the world for anyone to venture alone, Beah had always wanted to try his luck. Funny how, when he finally did leave the village, it was those same preachers who insisted he *must* now go, he must sacrifice himself for the good of the people.

Eamon was still talking. Beah shook his head and forced himself to focus on his companion's words.

"—so I agreed to teach him falconry. It was wild, how quickly I fell in love with him. If I didn't know better, I'd think he used mind control."

That caught Beah's attention. "The rin can control your mind?"

"W-well, yeah, the older ones. So I've heard, anyway."

"How old? How long do they live?"

"Centuries. Rafe is just shy of two hundred, and he's considered young."

Beah's mouth fell open. "How long do humans live?"

Eamon hummed. "Bound humans live as long as their rin companion lives. Unbound, less than a century."

"Hmm," Beah said, then, "so you're tied to a rin and will live for centuries."

"Yes. If I get back to him. I don't know if the magic works across worlds."

After a few moments' silent thought, Beah said, "Probably not. Each world is ruled by a different deity and has different rules." He poked his fingertip into the soil by his leg, cringing at the clingy wet texture, but continuing to poke at it anyway. "You quoted from the Rite of Devotion when we first met. Are you familiar with the Path of the Gods?"

To his surprise, Eamon recited the first few lines of the Path perfectly. "*Life starts in the hands of the mother, Mora, and in her care, we learn to walk and love. In our youth, we journey beside Prelis, who teaches us joy and strength.*"

Beah nodded and then realized in the darkness Eamon wouldn't be able to see him. "Yes. Each deity oversees one of our twelve lives."

"One stage of our life," Eamon said.

"No, we have twelve lives," Beah corrected. "*Shadelin is the last, the one who holds our frail hands as we tremble with the knowledge of the twelve and reach the end of our path.*"

"My preachers taught it differently."

"Well," Beah said, "this world is Shadelin's. This is the last on the path. For me to go with you to another world...I'd be spitting in the face of the gods. I'd be backtracking on my path. Cheating. Earning more time."

"I see." In the distance, something brayed in fear. Beah waited for silence again before he continued.

"They've spit in my face already," he said softly. "I came back to find you because I want to go with you. My father used to tell me we make our own paths. I thought he meant within each life, but perhaps he meant... something else. He disappeared when I was little. I wish I could ask him."

"I'm sorry."

"No need. I was young. Children are resilient."

They talked until the early light of dawn began to trickle through the branches and warm the forest. Eamon had been slouching further and further against Beah's shoulder as night progressed, and when birds began to sing and the blackness melted into gray, Beah let his companion doze off using his shoulder as a pillow.

Chapter Sixteen

EAMON

When morning came, Eamon bathed and washed his clothes. A spot of sun helped dry his breeches, but the process still set them behind by half a day—Eamon didn't mind though. After a thorough inspection of his injuries, Beah let him nap in a patch of grass. He was groggy when he first woke, but, once he'd eaten and dressed, Beah insisted they pack up and continue their journey.

Before long, they reached the place where the ghoul had attacked Eamon and found the tree had crushed the creature. Other animals had been at its body all night, feeding, and blackish-red bones jutted out through gaps in the flesh. What Eamon had thought was the thing bearing down on him with claws and weight had merely been branches of the tree scraping and striking him. He fetched his arrows from the ghoul's body, proud to see he'd hit the thing directly in the eye after all.

"Impressive," Beah said, watching Eamon tug the arrow free. "I guess the goddess Wesige favors you."

"I guess all the practice I put in favors me," Eamon replied with a smile and a wink. Beah made a half nod of agreement and smiled in return as Eamon cleaned the blood and gunk off his weapon with leaves and grass. Somehow, his bow had survived the impact from the tree. He would have to give Rafe's weaponsmith some kind of thank you gift when he returned home.

They continued on after the pause to reclaim his arrows, neither talking much. Eamon's head throbbed dully, so he had no desire to speak, and Beah was quiet by nature. The forest was still a comforting place to Eamon, but after the encounter last night, he was glad to have company. Especially company carrying a sword. Beah's loose-wrapped clothing wasn't as suited to forest travel as Eamon's tighter, heavier garments, and the other man fell behind frequently to untangle himself from the underbrush. The murderous expression on his face when Eamon laughed about it made Eamon laugh even harder, and when Beah let out a resigned sigh, it reminded Eamon so much of Rafe, he couldn't stop chuckling for an hour. Beah tolerated it with a sage patience that belied his age.

"You'll like Rafe," Eamon said after a while.

"What makes you say so?"

"He looks at me with the exact same long-suffering expressions you do."

Beah snorted. "Do you laugh at his frustrations too?"

"When they're funny." Eamon flashed a grin at his companion and got an eye roll in return.

His injuries from being struck and clawed by the branches of a falling tree were minor annoyances, barely noticeable as he walked, but late in the day, Eamon was overcome by a searing agony that drove him to the ground instantly. His leg—*his leg, oh gods*! A flaming blade straight to the bone from hip to knee, ripping through flesh and muscle as if they were no thicker than flower petals.

He screamed.

Beah was on his knees beside him in an instant. "Shh, Eamon! What happened? Are you hurt?"

He thrashed, gasping, hand pressed against the injury to steep the blood flow. Beah continued asking questions, but Eamon didn't hear him over his own sobs. What had happened? There hadn't been anything near his leg, certainly nothing to cause so much pain!

"What's *wrong*, Eamon?" Beah snapped, putting a hand on Eamon's thigh, pressing. "Is it your leg? What happened?"

"My leg," Eamon gasped. "Bleeding—"

"There is no blood, Eamon!"

What did he mean there was no blood? It was there, wet and hot against his thigh. He peeled his hand away from the fabric of his breeches and looked down, expecting to see his palm stained red and shiny, his breeches drenched in red-black blood...but Beah was right. There was no blood, and realization dawned.

"Rafe," he panted and struggled to find the place where his mind stopped and Rafe's began. He'd gotten in the habit lately of keeping their connection open and unguarded in a way he hadn't since they'd been newly bound and didn't know any better. He was desperate to receive any sort of sensation or indication of life from his lover. Now that he was getting one, with his mind so unguarded, it was overwhelming.

"What?" Beah asked.

They were still connected, despite the distance, despite the veil between their worlds. He tried to push his thoughts out along the bond. *Rafe, can you hear me? Are you all right?*

"*Eamon!*" Beah was shaking his shoulder.

Eamon drew in a sharp breath and forced his mind to the physical presence around him, subduing the pain to a manageable level. He might have closed it off altogether, but this was the first shimmer of Rafe he'd sensed in far too long. Irrational as it was, he wanted to cling to it.

"Beah," he gasped. "Rafe is hurt."

"What?"

"How far are we from your village?"

"Days," he said. "What do you mean Rafe is hurt? Are *you* okay?"

"We're bound. I—I can't reach him...but I experienced his pain."

"There's nothing you can do for him from here," Beah said. "I'm sorry. Are *you* hurt?"

Eamon swallowed, lying on the ground looking up at the leaves. He shook his head to answer Beah's question and fought the tightness in his throat and chest. He'd tried more than once to reach out to Rafe through their bond and hadn't managed. He assumed Rafe had done the same—unless Rafe thought him dead.

But they were still connected. They were still bound. Dizziness swept over him, and a sob wracked his body.

If he felt Rafe's pain, perhaps Rafe would feel his. He drew his dagger, threw his bond wide open again, and, before Beah could stop him, sliced the blade across his left arm, below the bend of his elbow. Hot, sharp pain sprang up as quick as the blood began to spill, but it was faint in the shadow of Rafe's pain. Eamon dropped his blade and drove his fingers against the wound to increase the pain until tears ran down his cheeks and the sob building in his chest escaped.

Beah grabbed his wrist and yanked his hand away from the wound. "What are you *doing*?"

"Saying hello," he whispered through a cringe.

"By cutting yourself?"

"If that's what it takes."

"You've lost your mind," Beah said, letting go of Eamon's wrist. He sat back in the grass and stared at Eamon with wide eyes. "Gods, I am a fool to have come after you."

"I just want him to know I'm alive," Eamon said and swallowed another sob.

The river was wide and sluggish there, and he walked to its shore and scooped cold water in one hand to clean his wound. Beah's footsteps crunched through the undergrowth behind him, but he didn't speak as Eamon washed the blood away.

After Eamon's wound was cleaned, Beah treated it with a salve and wrapped it in a relatively clean cloth.

"Don't do that again," he said, his voice low and serious. "They can smell a single drop of blood from a great distance. You'll attract them directly to us. We can't have another sleepless night tonight."

"I'm sorry," Eamon said, but they were empty words. It was impossible to stop smiling. In theory, Rafe was now aware he was alive. He'd just given the love of his life *hope*, and he would take any number of minor cuts and sleepless nights hiding from ghouls if it meant Rafe had hope.

"You are a lovesick fool," Beah muttered, running a hand over his face. "You'd better not get us killed."

They continued on, and though Eamon was tired and the dull pain remained in his thigh, he couldn't help but smile all day. The pain meant Rafe was alive. He took solace in it.

THE PAIN DIDN'T disappear completely for days, and while Eamon drew comfort from the reminder of Rafe's presence, he also found it worrisome. Rafe should have healed from any injury within a day if he was fed well. In Seacliff Manor, dozens of humans and even a few other rin were available and willing to serve as unbound feeders for their lord. Was Rafe no longer at the manor? Where would he go? Why wasn't he feeding? What had caused his injury in the first place? Eamon worried briefly it meant Rafe had died, but if their bond was still functional across whatever vast distance separated them, then he would likely have died as well. That was the true downside to the bond, and perhaps the only downside. With their lives bound together by the rin's magic, Eamon lived as long as his rin companion lived—be it five days, or five centuries.

He and Beah didn't speak much as they hiked, and they only took breaks to sleep and eat. The river was their constant companion until they reached the white tree and the tributary Beah had told Eamon to follow.

"I'm glad you're with me," Eamon said, looking at the tree with a frown. It did seem to be lighter brown than the rest of those around it, but not the stark white Eamon had expected. He might have missed it entirely and gotten lost in this godsforsaken place.

They hadn't encountered any more ghouls the past two nights, but had slept in shifts just in case. Beah's company helped ease Eamon's anxiety about what was to come, even though the other man was not talkative or particularly reassuring when he did speak. He seemed caught up in his own mind, and Eamon couldn't blame him. In just a few days, they would be back in the village where he'd been sentenced to death, and there was no telling what would happen.

They camped by the intersection of the tributary and river that night, both quietly lost in their own thoughts. Eamon took the first watch, and Beah curled up under a blanket and was asleep within seconds. One good thing about long, hard journeys—the exhaustion was an excellent lullaby.

The sounds of the forest kept Eamon company as he paced to stay awake. He heard ghouls and other animals in the distance, but nothing close enough to worry him. One night, he'd seen the flash of red eyes on the far side of the river, but when he frantically woke Beah, he reassured him the river was wide and deep enough to keep the creatures at bay. It was only if they were on this side of the river he had to worry.

He pulled off his boots, soaking his sore feet in the cool water, mulling over the situation. He'd gone on long hunting excursions before, no one but him, his falcon, a horse, and a few companions, but other than the journey from his home village to Seacliff, he'd never had an "adventure" quite like this. He preferred his adventures on paper, bound between covers and easy to end when he needed a break. When he was young, he'd yearned for excitement, to see the world, but he didn't like the fear that came along with it. Adventure like a few nights in the safe woods outside Seacliff, sure. Adventure like flirtation with a being who might suck his life out in exchange for the most amazing orgasm he'd ever experience, yes. As he got older, he learned those were the adventures he wanted.

This "hiking through an unfamiliar forest far from home, separated from everything he loved" adventure was horseshit, and when he returned to Seacliff, he wasn't going to leave the manor house for days. Maybe he wouldn't even leave his bed. Maybe he'd have adventures with Rafe, adventures like "what happens if I put my tongue here?" or "how many times can he come in one night?"

Eamon scooted back and stretched his legs out over the grass to let his feet dry. He flopped down to stare up at the stars through an opening in the canopy and tentatively opened his mind to Rafe. The pain in his leg had faded to virtually nothing, even when he was fully accepting of all sensation through the bond. The pain in his arm remained and would remain until his slow human body knitted itself together.

As he lay, wiggling his toes and trying to pick out anything familiar in the stars above him, a sudden surge of *need* made him gasp and immediately grow hard. Like the pain that had hit his leg a few days ago, the sensation belonged to Rafe, and Eamon was just experiencing it secondhand. It made him smile, the familiarity of the *other's* need like an embrace he desperately wanted. He didn't know if Rafe was alone or with someone, but he hoped for the former as he silenced a moan.

They'd play a game like this sometimes, trying to make the other get off only through the secondhand sensations of what they were doing to themselves. Eamon glanced at Beah—still sleeping—and then relaxed to bask in the sensation. It was difficult to be far away and unable to communicate coherent thoughts, but if the bond was going to let them share the most basic sensations, pain and pleasure, then Eamon would do as much as possible with it, and he suspected Rafe would do the same until they were together again.

Pleasure zipped around his chest, and Eamon closed his eyes to picture Rafe standing naked by the bed, thumbs grazing over his nipples. He teased his own nipples in response, hoping Rafe felt his answer and knew he was listening. The pleasure centered on his cock then, and Eamon pushed his breeches down and rubbed a hand over himself, his body hard under his palm. Everything was amplified by the shared pleasure of his lover's touch, and Eamon forgot where he was, forgot his predicament, forgot everything but playing follow-the-leader across his body until it became unbearable, and he brought himself off with a few quick, hard tugs on his cock. Rafe's climax echoed his seconds later, and Eamon smiled as the aftershocks shivered through him. *I'm here.*

The words were lost in the distance somewhere, but it still comforted him to think them, like whispering to his lover while he slept. Rafe couldn't hear it, but Eamon liked to say the words anyway. *I'm alive. I'm going to come home to you. I love you.*

Chapter Seventeen

EAMON

Since Beah rarely spoke, Eamon learned to read his body language. When the trees began to thin and they approached the upper arm of the mountains where Beah's village was located, Beah's pace slowed. He glanced around more, called for more breaks, and at the edge of the trees when the only thing separating them from the mountains was a half-day-long hike across familiar red stone, he suggested they camp.

"We can reach the mountains by nightfall," Eamon said. They were so close to...to something. To people. To this Alma, who might be able to help.

"It would be best to wait for the gatherers to find us. The village is well hidden. If we find it ourselves, it'll be suspicious."

"The gatherers?"

"Foragers. The only people permitted to leave the village."

"When will they come?"

"I'm not certain."

Eamon groaned. "Can we go closer, so they'll see us out in the open?"

"Eamon."

"We're almost there, Beah!"

"*Eamon*." The smaller man's dark eyes turned up to him, and he had to clench his fist to calm the surge of frustration. Beah was his guide. He was young, and he was scared.

"Sorry." A deep breath stretched his lungs and calmed his nerves. "Sorry. I'm just…I miss Rafe."

"I've noticed." Beah's dry tone said he knew exactly what Eamon had been doing every night.

Eamon's face flushed. It was a miracle his rutting hadn't attracted any curious animals. Or hungry ones.

"Sorry," he said again. "I can feel him. Like the pain…except…"

"Yes," Beah said flatly, "I understand."

Eamon ducked his head in embarrassment, mumbled something about filling their waterskins, and headed for the stream. The water here was shallow, trickling across the stony streambed, so it took Eamon several minutes to fill his waterskin. The scuff of boots on stone behind him announced Beah's company. He stepped over the narrow stream and squatted to fill his own waterskin.

"When we arrive," he said slowly, "it would be best if I can stay silent and keep my face hidden. I'm meant to be dead. My being alive will cast suspicion on the priestess. The priestess who might be able to help you."

"Yes, of course." Eamon pursed his lips thoughtfully. "Perhaps we can say you are my travelling companion. We met in the forest. You saved me from a morroul—"

Beah lifted a hand. "They are servants of Shadelin. If I attacked one, I am a heretic. You don't want them to think that."

Eamon swore under his breath. They *worshipped* those monsters. Really, truly believed they were godsends. "You were defending yourself. I was defending myself. They truly think if one attacks you, you should just *accept it*?"

"This is the final world. All must die."

"Then why did you...I mean, you avoided death. You've killed and eaten them."

"*You* killed it."

"You carved up its body and dried its meat."

Beah made a face but didn't dispute it. Eamon let the topic drop. He'd pushed his nervous host enough.

The stream trickled over Eamon's fingers, the water warmed by the expanse of open ground it had crossed to reach them. He set his filled waterskin aside and cupped his hands to gather water to splash his face. Beah got up and left once his waterskin was full, and Eamon followed on his heels.

"What can I expect when we make it to the village?" he asked when they'd settled into the shelter of the trees. From the sound of things, telling the truth was not the best approach, at least with the villagers. Perhaps to the elders or preachers, or this priestess. The thought of going into this unfamiliar setting with unfamiliar people and lying his ass off made his stomach twist and roll.

"They are cautious people," Beah said. "Visitors are not common. You'll be asked a lot of questions."

"Are they generous though?"

Beah sipped from his waterskin and looked away. "It is good manners to welcome guests to our hearths."

The words jangled at something deep in Eamon's memory, and he quoted, "'There is no greater godliness than showing mercy to those in need.'"

It was a verse from the book of the deities, one of the most sacred tenets of the worship of the twelve. His companion smiled, but a confused expression showed in lines around his eyes.

"It is interesting how you know so much of my ways if you are from another world."

"All the worlds used to trade," Eamon said. "Goods, labor, ideas. I guess your world and mine used to trade too. It's still a practiced religion in most of my world. Except...without the morroul worshipping."

Beah smiled a little. "If you don't have morroul in your world, then that makes sense."

"We have them," Eamon said. "They trespass into our world, which is how I ended up here. They can tear the veil and travel the worlds."

"Can they?"

"Yes. They've been doing it for years around Seacliff."

"Maybe if Alma can't help, you can find a morroul that will." Beah smirked, but Eamon frowned at him.

"Maybe it'll eat me and then go to Seacliff. I'd end up at home, just...in its belly."

"That would be unfortunate."

Eamon had to laugh, even though nothing about the situation was particularly funny. His only options lately were to panic, or to laugh, and he was trying to stick with the latter.

"What should I tell the villagers when they ask questions? I can't tell them I came from another world, can I?"

"You can," Beah said. "They might not believe you, and they might not trust you, but it may be safer to err on the side of honesty since you don't know this world well enough to lie about it."

Eamon nodded.

"They likely won't trust you no matter what you tell them," Beah said. "Remember the two visitors I told you about? The traveler and the herbalist?"

"Yes."

"The second one, herbalist woman? The villagers drove her out because she was trying to teach a way of...repelling morroul. There's a scent, she said, which they hate. The elders threw her out for sacrilege."

"Oh." Eamon's brows went up. He was going to have to be very careful with what he said. He hated ghouls and nothing would change his loathing. He wasn't sure he'd be able to lie about it. Best to avoid the topic altogether. "Do you think they will take us to the priestess immediately?"

"No," Beah said with a sigh. "She is the one closest to the god. They may not take us to see her at all. We can't tell them why we want to see her either. We may have to sneak."

"Why *do* we want to see her?" Eamon asked. "You said you'd never seen or known anyone to create portals. What's so special about this woman?"

Beah fell silent again, and Eamon frowned. The boy sure liked to evade questions. Eamon was about to push him when he spoke.

"The night I was to be sacrificed. I told you I panicked."

"Yes. I would have too."

Beah scoffed but didn't debate. "When I heard the morroul coming, this...eerie sense of calm filled me. I realized I wasn't supposed to die there, and I started climbing. The things came into the pit, three of them, but they started fighting each other, and I managed to get to the top. Alma was there, chanting, and the morroul were fighting, and then...suddenly there was nothing."

"Nothing?" Eamon echoed.

"Nothing. The morroul were gone. Then Alma saw me and said...a lot of words priestesses shouldn't use. She took me to her hut, gave me food and water and my clothes and sword, and told me if I wanted to live, I ought to leave. Stay near the water. Never return. So that's what I did. I don't know what any of it means. It didn't matter, honestly. I was never going to go back."

Eamon frowned, staring at the stream as the water bubbled past. This Alma priestess might be able to make portals. Humans were the only ones able to do so in his world. It would make sense if humans from other worlds were able to as well. His anxiety was mounting though. It was good Beah had told him not to lie about everything—he was a terrible liar. Still, this would be a strange situation, and he and Beah were going to be the ones in a vulnerable position. Especially Beah.

"Rest," Beah said. He waved a hand toward the trees they'd come from. "Go...communicate with your lover." He smiled, and Eamon's ears warmed with a sudden blush.

"I'm sorry."

"Don't be. I'm glad you can reach him. You've been calmer."

That was true. Since realizing he and Rafe were still bound, he'd become more confident. For some reason, he'd been afraid his level-headed lover would do something foolish in his absence. Probably a silly fear, but he was full of silly fears. This was one less he had to worry about.

Chapter Eighteen

RAFE

"This is foolish, my lord."

"I know."

They had been forced to return to the manor after Rafe's close call with the ghoul. Kourt and Sier deserved proper funerals, and Rafe needed time to recover. As it turned out, the injury had been the best thing to happen to him since Eamon's disappearance. In the moment, he'd thought the phantom pain in his arm had been a hallucination, but when he decided to test his theory at home in the privacy of his bed, and phantom hands followed his movements, he'd been relieved enough to cry. Wherever Eamon was, he was alive, and their bond had not been broken.

But there was a ghoul sighting in the village, and Rafe, Kiran, and a handful of others had ridden out to capture it.

"If you're going to get in its head this time," Kiran said softly, "perhaps give us a moment's warning."

"I'm going to get in its head. I'm going to get in every ghoul's head until I find the one that can get me Eamon back."

"I'm not sure it's safe, my lord."

Something had changed in Kiran when Rafe was injured. It was there the next time he fed on him. The dedication, loyalty, and respect he'd always had for Rafe had been joined by something else, something Rafe had sensed in others, but never from Kiran.

Romantic love.

It was a risk expected with humans—the conflation of sexual pleasure and love—he had hoped to avoid with Kiran. He suspected the emotion had been there for a while, underneath the devotion and obedience, and its surfacing had more to do with his blood spilling all over the grass than it did with him driving Kiran to orgasm a dozen or more times since Eamon had disappeared. Still, he wasn't sure what to do with it, so for now he chose to ignore it.

"We'll restrain it properly this time, first," Rafe said. "I'll enter its mind only after it can't harm me."

"We don't understand much about them though. What if they can enter *your* mind?"

That was a horrifying thought. What if? They clearly had some degree of magic if they were able to create portals—which they had to be able to do if they were able to throw Eamon into another world. The images Rafe had pulled from the ghoul's mind days ago had him second-guessing everything he thought he understood about them. What if the human had sent *all* those ghouls through? What if none of them had magic? But then, how had Eamon gone through to another world? None of it made sense, so he chose to continue believing as he always had. Ghouls had magic, and he was going to find one to get him through to Eamon.

"I'll be fine," Rafe assured his companion, and that was the end of the discussion.

The ghoul that had been sighted near the village was a hellacious thing, shaggy and dog-like, but enormous.

They kept their distance this time, filling it full of arrows, bleeding it into weakness. It was a long, slow process. By the time the thing seemed weak enough to approach, the entire hunting party was as exhausted.

They got it hobbled in chains and collared, three of the strongest holding chains on each side of its neck, before Rafe approached. He met its eyes from a distance—dark spheres poking up through red, puffy lids—and forced himself against its mind. This ghoul, though less humanoid than the last, had more conscious control over its mind. It pushed back. Rafe swore. He stood his ground alone, his companions engaged in controlling the tired and bleeding creature's body. If they lost control, it would only take a quick lunge from the ghoul's powerful haunches, and it would snap Rafe up and bite him in half.

He pushed harder, and the thing's exhaustion gave way to his anger and determination. Its thoughts filled his mind, and he shoved one of his own at it. *Stop fighting.*

Outside his mind, he was vaguely aware of it going limp, sinking into a prone position. He stepped closer, thinking calm thoughts, ignoring the tension in the air around him. Calm thoughts. His hand came in contact with its furred cheek, and he dove deeper.

Hunger.

Emptiness.

From the memories Rafe had seen in the previous ghoul's mind, he assumed their world was a wasteland. Ghouls were solitary and territorial—he'd determined as much when the ghoul had seen others coming toward its human prey, but it had been too hungry to fight them until they were an immediate threat. Most of their lives were spent prowling, hunting, fighting. Most of their prey was small, not satisfying. Humans were large and delicious, but hard to find, and always in groups, always fighting.

Good. If Eamon ended up with those humans, at least he'd be protected.

Rafe pushed a thought at the ghoul. *How did you get here?*

The memory flooded his senses. A cavern, high-ceilinged and lit with strange glowing plants. A pale man—no, not a human. It smelled wrong. It looked human, but smelled...other. The ghoul hadn't realized what it was, but Rafe did. *Rin.* What was happening? Rin and ghouls were mortal enemies. For this ghoul to let a rin near it without trying to tear it limb from limb... But there was a familiarity there. The rin smiled and lay a hand on the ghoul's cheek, much as Rafe was doing now, and pushed a memory into the ghoul's mind. A forest. A field. A village. And an order.

"Go. Eat. Return."

And the ghoul...obeyed.

Rafe rode along the creature's memories as it turned placidly away from the rin. And a flowing, charging *something* built inside it, much like when Rafe gathered his strength to take control of a mind. The ghoul lifted a paw and drove the something—the magic—forward, sliced through the air, and its claws left shimmering trails. It clawed again and again, tearing a hole. It climbed through, and Rafe recognized the scenery. It looked across a field toward Seacliff village. Its nostrils flared. *Eat. Return.*

A rin giving orders to a ghoul, and the ghoul obeying, threw Rafe's mind into turmoil. They were supposed to hate each other. They were supposed to be mortal enemies, competitors. What was a rin doing in the ghoul's world?

His placid subject stirred under his hand, and he shoved the thoughts aside to double his focus on the ghoul. He was *not* going to die due to his own distraction. The ghoul's master did not matter right now. What mattered right now was Eamon, and how the ghouls were traveling between worlds. They clearly had the same ability as humans. Rafe dug through its memories—it had traveled many times, between points of its own world, and, occasionally, into Rafe's world at the order of the mysterious rin. Its memories told him it had come through only hours before.

He wondered if the tear was still there. He wondered what it would take to create one of his own.

The ghoul's exhaustion had lowered its guard, and Rafe had no trouble digging through its mind for anything that might prove useful. Memories of its life drowned him, overwhelming him with knowledge and images he didn't understand. When he'd had enough, Rafe focused deeper, outside the mind and into the essence of the creature's life. Much like any other living thing, energy swirled through it like water eddying around a brook, flowing perpetually from heart and mind to every fiber of its body. Tentatively, Rafe dipped into the flow and drew it into himself. Rin were able to feed on any animal life. Humans were prized far and above all else for their complexity and companionship, for their ability to understand and give consent. He doubted the last bit had anything to do with the ghouls' taste for human flesh.

But the ghoul had lots of life in its large body, and when Rafe tugged its life into himself, a warm breath of power came with it. He pulled in more, deepening the connection between them. The creature growled, but he'd dug into its mind with his own, and forced its submission as he drained it. This was not the kind of feeding he was used to. He'd never taken without consent, without providing something in return. As he pulled more and more from the creature's body, he realized, for the first time, he was going to experience death. He was going to drain every shred of life, of energy and magic, feel its mind shut off and its heart stop beating.

He shuddered but didn't stop.

The life filled him with more strength than he'd ever possessed before. His muscles hardened, his heart pounded and his every sense transcended belief. Even as he stood engaged with the ghoul's mind, he became acutely aware of Kiran, of his other guards—their sweat, the trembling of their muscles, the smell of their fear. Whispered voices.

"What is he doing?"

"Is that safe?"

"Should we stop him?"

And through all of it, the spark of the ghoul's life grew dimmer, until he'd emptied its body and its mind disappeared completely. He stumbled backward as if he'd been pulling on a rope with all his strength and it suddenly came free of its anchor.

"My lord." Kiran was beside him in an instant.

The whispers continued.

"He killed it."

"He drained it to death."

"I didn't know that was possible."

Power coursed through him like a river pounding through a streambed. He was certain he was glowing with energy, shaking all over with the need to *do something.* Kill. Eat. Fuck. Tear.

He focused on the ghoul's memories, on the place it had spent most of its time. He thought of the growing tension and heat pulsing through its limbs as it gathered its magic to tear a hole in the world. Rafe had its magic now. It was different from his own, coarser and hotter, yet familiar enough he trusted his instincts to wield it.

Stepping away from his entourage, he curled his fingers into a claw and *tore*. Not just with his physical movement, but with his mind, with his energy. A shimmer followed his hand, and he let out a shout.

I'm coming, Eamon.

Chapter Nineteen

EAMON

The village watch did not come the first night, or the next morning, so Beah reluctantly agreed to take Eamon straight into the village. As with the "white tree," Eamon was hugely relieved Beah was with him to find the rock outcropping "shaped like a boot," because he'd never seen such a deformed boot in his life.

"You've got a powerful imagination in that head of yours," he muttered to his companion.

Beah had been traveling with his hair and face covered all day, hood up, as perfectly nondescript as possible. They'd settled on telling the truth about where Eamon was from but decided to try including Beah in the story as if he, too, came from Eamon's world. Beah was going to play mute, out of fear his voice would give him away if he spoke. He'd left his sword in the trees too—it would give him away as surely as his face and voice, he'd said. But his eyes had lingered on it for a long time after he wedged it in the split of an old oak, and kept wandering toward it until they'd gone too far for him to be subtle about it.

A twinge of regret pricked at Eamon's heart. The village had tried to put Beah to death, and Eamon expected him to return there. It was a lot to ask, but Beah was handling it all without complaint. Rafe would like him, Eamon decided. Once they returned to Seacliff, he looked forward to his two-century-old lover meeting this quiet young man.

They'd spent some time during the walk covering details about Beah's village—things Eamon should know for his own safety but had to pretend not to. Who to respect, how to act, and so on. Eamon was doing his best to remain calm.

"Last chance for questions before I stop talking," Beah said.

Eamon asked the question he'd been afraid of since the moment Beah returned to him in the forest. "What if someone recognizes you?"

It seemed Beah wasn't going to answer for some time. His eyes, the only part of him left uncovered, turned down, then up and away, before he finally said, "Let's just make sure that doesn't happen."

That was not encouraging at all. Eamon took a deep breath and let it out slowly to calm his pounding heart. "Very well."

"You can do this," Beah said, laying a friendly hand on Eamon's shoulder. "You just need to convince them we're harmless and get us through the day. At night, we can sneak out to visit Alma. If she can help, then you'll be sleeping in your own bed tonight."

"Yes," Eamon said, letting out another slow breath. His own bed sounded wonderful. His bed, with Rafe in his arms, in his body, in his mind. He wanted to open himself to his lover, to give himself to him completely, lose himself in the safety and strength Rafe provided. "All right. Let's go."

The climb to the village was treacherous. Eamon wondered how often people made the journey. If they had access to water other than the stream below. He thought to ask Beah but saved his breath. Beah had fallen silent and wouldn't be speaking again until they were safely out of his village. Eamon's curiosity would have to remain unsatisfied.

After a near-eternity of zigs and zags, they squeezed through a narrow opening and stepped out into a wide, flat canyon floor housing more life than Eamon had seen since his arrival in this world. Not only human life, but animals and plants. The place they'd entered was above the village, giving them a view of about fifty small mud-brick houses in vague circles around a central well and what appeared to be a raised platform for meetings. As Eamon descended to the village, a sharp voice halted him.

"Who are you?"

A man shoved aside the thick woven hanging that covered the doorway of the nearest building and came out holding a crude sword similar to the one Beah had carried. He wore clothing also similar to Beah's—loose, draped robes in natural shades, but didn't have his hood up or face covered. He was brown-skinned and older, hair graying at the temples, his wrinkled face stuck in a scowl. Eamon put his hands up immediately, and Beah followed suit.

"Travelers," Eamon said. Beah had warned him to keep it simple unless it became necessary to express more.

"*Travelers*," the man said, sneering. Eamon's brows went up. Skepticism and distrust, he expected. Derision, though? That was harsh. For a village that only averaged one or two visitors every generation, surely it wouldn't ruin them to be more accepting.

"Yes," Eamon said. "We mean no harm."

Another man came out of the hut on their right—sword sheathed, at least. There were men remaining in each of the huts as well, training arrows on them through the windows. Gods, Beah had really understated the village's distrust of strangers.

"We'll see about that," the first man said.

"I sent Jacob to the elders," the second said in a lowered voice. Beyond them, a young kid darted through the red stone streets. He disappeared into one of the larger buildings.

"How'd you find us?" the first man demanded, coming closer with his sword pointed at them.

Eamon resisted the urge to step back. Being Rafe's companion gave him some degree of authority and respect around the manor. Not much—he lacked the experience, heritage, or power to be truly respectable—but it was more than he'd ever had before. It had taken him a long time to get used to people nodding in deference to him in corridors and the village proper, even with Rafe constantly reassuring him he was worthy of their respect. Eamon took a deep breath and sought the part of him accustomed to being seen as an authority figure.

"I believe I'll wait for the elders to ask me questions before I answer anything," Eamon said simply, hands still in the air.

"Arrogant—"

"Fools!" A man's voice cut sharply over the guard's next word, and he immediately jumped and turned. Not much of a guard, if he was willing to put his back to his "captives."

Eamon turned toward the voice as well, relaxing his shoulders. He guessed this was the "eldest," the leader of the village. Whether he was leader because he was truly the eldest, or if it was some misnomer of a title, Eamon hadn't bothered to ask Beah. Watching as the man approached, the title certainly seemed accurate. His face was covered in mountains and canyons, wrinkles deep enough to get lost in, cheekbones protruding like plateaus from a wasteland. A woman followed him, younger, but not by much, and a man even younger followed her. All had brown skin and dark hair, brown eyes, and wore loose clothing in neutral shades.

"Is this any way to treat our first visitors in ages?" the eldest asked. Despite his apparent age, his voice didn't waver or creak like Eamon's grandfather's voice always had before he passed. The eldest brushed past the guards and came straight up to Eamon before offering a bow, which Eamon and Beah returned. "Greetings, strangers. I am Haroun, the eldest. This is my daughter, Ava, and Sharim, our head priest."

"It's an honor to meet you," Eamon said, bowing slightly again. "I am Eamon, and this is my companion, Daniel. We are travelers." They had discussed what name Eamon should give for Beah. After confessing "Beah" was not his given name, the young man nevertheless insisted on choosing another one altogether.

The eldest gazed at Eamon with narrowed eyes, scanning him from head to toe. Eamon held his breath. His skin color would raise questions, perhaps even suspicion or distrust, but there was no way to avoid it.

"Come," Haroun said, finally. "You must be tired. We will have a meal prepared while we talk."

Eamon and Beah followed Haroun, Ava, and Sharim to the large building the child had disappeared into earlier. Inside, it became apparent this was some kind of meeting hall. Rugs and cushions lay scattered about the floor. Nothing was made of wood. There were no tables, no chairs. The eldest settled on one of the cushions with some assistance from his daughter, and Sharim followed his lead. Eamon and Beah did as well, but Ava walked to the far side of the meeting room and disappeared through a doorway.

"You must forgive the men you met outside," Haroun said. "We are not accustomed to visitors, and you are quite a strange sight."

"It's all right," Eamon said, offering a smile.

"Tell me, where are you from, Eamon?"

Eamon hesitated, but Beah had advised him to go with the truth, so he took the plunge. "We are from another world. We came here by accident a few weeks ago."

The eldest studied him for the space of several heartbeats, face expressionless, before he said, "We had a visitor from another world many, many seasons ago."

"We aren't common," Eamon said and tried to smile, but it was quickly apparent this old man had no interest in humor.

"Why are you here? How did you find us?"

"Misfortune to the first question, luck to the second."

"Explain."

Eamon hesitated. He couldn't confess to fighting a ghoul, but an outright lie was too risky. To avoid trouble, he merely said, "I don't understand it myself. One minute I was home, and the next I was in the desert."

The eldest turned his eyes to Beah. "And you?"

"He doesn't speak," Eamon said quickly. "It's his way." It amused him to think that in reality, it wasn't far from the truth. His companion was far from talkative.

"I see." The old man looked suspicious but didn't press.

Ava returned with a tray, offering both of them cups of water and a thin, flat bread with fruit. Eamon had practically forgotten the taste and texture of bread and had to suppress a moan when he bit into it. The conversation paused as they ate. Beah politely declined all food and water, and Eamon made a note to make sure he drank as soon as they were alone.

Before he'd even finished his piece of bread, Eamon became aware of...something else. Something tickled at the part of his mind usually full of Rafe's life and thoughts and emotions. It wasn't pain, and it wasn't pleasure... It was dizzying, though, and he swayed. The hand he threw out to catch himself knocked over his cup of water with a clatter.

"Eamon?" the eldest said, leaning forward, his fluffy gray brows pulled together in concern.

Eamon shook his head. "I apologize. It's been a long journey."

"Ava," the eldest called, and she appeared. "Find someone willing to house our guests for the night."

"Yes, Father." She headed out the way they'd come in.

The world spun and swam and shook, and Eamon covered his mouth in fear he was about to throw up. It wasn't pain or pleasure he was getting from Rafe. It was *power*—more power than he'd ever known his lover to possess. It was too much. It filled his mind, deafening him to his companions' speech. He tried to get up, mumbling something about needing air, but as soon as he pushed up from his seated position, he collapsed. Everything around him turned into a haze of movement, but he just stared at the ceiling of the hut until his mind shut off completely and everything went black.

Chapter Twenty

BEAH

"What is wrong with him?" the eldest demanded, but Beah merely shook his head. He knelt over Eamon, hands on his shoulder and arm, but Eamon seemed unaware of him. His blue eyes stared up at the ceiling without seeing, and his body was limp.

Being in his home village again, seeing familiar faces, had Beah's heart racing. He'd seen Eamon go into a panic a couple times since they met, and for the first time, Beah truly understood. Merely setting eyes on his village had left him nauseous and weak, barely able to keep himself upright and breathing.

And now Eamon was ill, leaving Beah to fend for himself.

Beah wanted to run, to flee screaming into the mountains and never see another human again. He would live out his life in a cave and eat lizards and cactus fruits until the day he died, be that tomorrow or twenty years from now. *Just don't speak and don't uncover your face,* he reminded himself as Sharim came closer to check on Eamon. Beah shuffled back, out of Sharim's way.

He remembered the holy man's eyes the day when Beah had reached into the pouch to draw his tile for the lottery. Contempt and satisfaction. His face had haunted Beah for days as he went through the pre-sacrifice cleansing rituals. Contempt. The gods were meant to treat all men equally, and godly men were too. But this one did not. This one hated Beah.

"What have you brought into the village?" Sharim demanded.

It took everything in Beah to pretend to be someone else—not the young girl he'd appeared as all his life but a stranger, a grown man traveling across worlds with his companion. A stranger who didn't speak, didn't shrilly defend himself or cry or beg, no matter how much he'd been conditioned to do so in his life. He shook his head again, quick and panicked, and Sharim scoffed and helped the eldest to his feet.

"You should leave, Haroun," he said, guiding the old man toward the door. "I will take care of this."

Beah wondered if Sharim had said something similar to the village leader before the last lottery, when Beah's strange behavior had become too much. *I will take care of this.*

No, Beah didn't think he wanted Sharim taking care of *anything.* He slapped Eamon's cheek once and then a second time even harder. It earned him a soft noise and fluttering eyelashes, but nothing more. Sharim had led Haroun to the door. He would return soon.

"Come on, Eamon," Beah whispered, shaking his companion. Eamon groaned and started trembling. Sharim was returning already. Beah grabbed Eamon's arm and yanked him into a sitting position.

"I've sent a runner to the medic. You shouldn't move him."

The medic! *No!*

Beah remembered countless times when a child had shown up at the door to collect his mother for some emergency or another—a birth, a death, an injury, a fever. He'd always worried when it happened. If the sick person wasn't able to come to her, but she had to go to them, it was serious. This was not...this *could not* be that serious. He hauled Eamon to his feet, sort of, heart racing from stress and exertion. The larger man flopped lifelessly, his height making it impossible for Beah to get him fully upright. Tears blurred Beah's vision. He'd been wary but willing to return home as long as Eamon controlled the situation, as long as they only stayed one day. This was not what he wanted. This was not what he'd expected.

"Where do you think you're taking him?" Sharim asked, stepping forward, holding up a hand. "The medic is on her way. Do you understand me?"

No. Maybe if he convinced himself he didn't understand Sharim's words, he'd make a believable act out of it without Eamon there to speak for him. Beah made it a handful of steps, Eamon's weight challenging his balance, every movement a labor, before the door opened again.

"Lay him down," Sharim said to Beah, voice sharp, and turned his attention to the woman who'd entered.

Beah froze in place at the sight of his mother, his legs too weak to take another step. His grip on Eamon's wrist slipped, the weight pulled him off balance, and he sank to his knees awkwardly, lowering Eamon to the cushions on the floor. Mellory crossed the room after a few soft words with Sharim and knelt beside Beah. Her attentive brown eyes focused on her patient, but Beah pulled his hood further down, shading his face as much as possible.

He wanted to ask questions—what was she finding as she touched Eamon's cheeks and looked into his eyes?—but he didn't dare to speak.

"Tell me what happened," Mellory said, and Sharim recounted the events of the morning. To his credit, he gave an accurate account and Beah didn't need to butt in. Nothing Sharim had said could have caused Eamon's collapse. Beah knew it, and his mother would realize it too. Eamon groaned softly but didn't rouse out of his stupor. "What has he eaten recently?"

Beah kept his face down and shook his head.

"This one doesn't speak," Sharim said.

"Oh." His mother's gaze was on him, on the side of his hood, curious and skeptical. "Well, there's nothing more I can do here. Can you get him to the sick house?"

The sick house. Practically a prison—a quarantined room near the edge of the village where mysterious illnesses were left to heal or worsen in peace. They didn't have much choice, though. Beah shrugged Eamon's arm onto his shoulder again, and Sharim took the other arm. The height difference between them meant Sharim took the majority of Eamon's weight, but Beah wasn't going to complain. His heart was racing, his head swam, and his eyes refused to focus.

They made it to the sick house with nothing more than curious stares to interfere with their passage. A couple children trailed behind them at a safe distance. Beah had always been kept away from the sick house, but as a curious kid, he'd peered through the window a few times. From the inside, it appeared as he expected—a pallet bed against one wall, a low table against the other, a cushion between the two for visitors. Wall hangings made a sad attempt at brightening the space, but somehow misery seemed to cling to it.

Eamon grunted when they lowered him gracelessly to the bed on the floor.

"He's reacting," Mellory said. "That's a good sign. He is aware of his body." She turned to Beah, and he lowered his head to stare at Eamon intently.

"Do you understand me... I'm sorry, what's his name?"

Sharim answered. "Daniel."

"Daniel. Nod if you understand me."

Beah nodded, still focused downward. His trembling hands threatened to give away his nerves, so he clenched them into fists.

His mother knelt at Eamon's side, and Beah turned his head away, terrified his mother would recognize him, and, somehow, also terrified she wouldn't. She was his mother, after all.

Mellory called out to the child who'd followed them to the sick house, demanding water and supplies. Beah stepped away, putting his back against the wall to watch from a short distance. Eamon's eyes had fallen closed, and he stirred every few minutes as if caught in a bad dream.

"He is feverish," Mellory murmured, her hand pressed to Eamon's forehead. She began working his buckles loose, much as Beah had done not long ago when he'd found Eamon in the desert. He was struck with a strange urge to slap her hands away, to put himself between Eamon and the woman who'd raised him. The woman who'd allowed him to be chosen as a sacrifice.

He wanted to run. But for Eamon, he stayed where he was until his mother finished tending her patient. She gave Eamon a yellowish tea, and the other man coughed as he swallowed it. Beah wrinkled his nose in sympathy—he'd had her fever-breaker tea before, and it tasted about as pleasant as a mouthful of dirt. But Eamon still didn't wake.

"The most I can do is keep the fever under control," Mellory said. "He's responding, so he's not too far gone yet."

She turned and looked up at Beah, a comforting smile in place—and their eyes met.

And she gasped. Beah looked away, a cold sweat breaking out over his whole body, but his mother had seen his eyes, and she recognized him.

She said his name. His old name. His birth name. And then Sharim knew too.

Beah fled. Out the open door, knocking a child out of the way as he went. He ran the way they'd come in.

"Stop her!" Sharim shouted from close behind him, but Beah didn't dare glance over his shoulder to see how close. Fear drove him in a wild sprint toward the edge of the village.

The guards who had challenged them when they arrived were running toward him, and Beah tried to change directions, but Sharim caught his sleeve and pulled, and Beah went off balance and fell to one knee. His hand went to his sword, only to remember he'd left it behind to avoid being recognized. A lot of good that had done. Sharim pulled his hood down, and Beah fought to keep the scarves around his face, noises of anger and fear leaving him—*high* noises, *feminine* noises. He sobbed.

Out there, surviving on his own, he'd been able to be the man he'd always known himself to be.

Here, he was just a girl, a troublesome child who acted strangely and wouldn't do anything she was supposed to do.

"You're supposed to be dead," Sharim snapped. He looked up. A small crowd had formed around them. He pointed at someone—"Go fetch Alma. Go! Hurry!"—and a man ran from the village center.

Sharim pulled Beah to his feet and jerked his arms behind him. Someone wrapped rope about his wrists, and he didn't fight.

Chapter Twenty-One

RAFE

The most jarring part of passing through the portal was going from grassy dusk to dusty stone and glaring sunlight. Rafe nearly cried out at the shock, hypersensitive pupils contracting so fast his head spun, feet stumbling at the change in texture. He pulled the hood up on his cloak and shaded his eyes with a gloved hand.

A scuffling noise behind him made him spin around, his hand dropping to his sword hilt—and then relaxing as Kiran appeared from the shimmering air. His reaction was the same as Rafe's, except he actually did let out a strangled noise of surprise before covering his eyes completely. Rafe's relief at realizing the scuffling noise wasn't a ghoul washed away when he realized the implications of this development.

"You shouldn't have followed me," he said.

Kiran scoffed, and Rafe had to smile. He should have known his retainer wouldn't let him simply disappear.

"Is everyone else coming too?"

"No. Just me. They're returning to the manor to tell Orienna what happened."

"Good." Rafe surveyed their surroundings. They were in some kind of quarry, a huge pit with gray stone walls rising on every side. Rafe had knowledge of the area from the ghoul's memories. There was a cave nearby where it had usually slept, and it liked to prowl around the top of the quarry, trying to spot any unsuspecting prey. The thought made him shiver and peer up. Rafe was not going to be unsuspecting prey for any ghoul.

"My lord, please tell me what happened back there. You're...overwhelmingly strong in my mind right now."

Overwhelming. Yes, that was probably the best word for Rafe's current state. The memories from the ghoul, the information he'd sussed out of its brain—there was some kind of hierarchy, a being of power who gave orders to these creatures—was overwhelming enough without the addition of the being's entire life force flowing through his body and mind. He wanted to rip, tear, eat, fuck, fight. He wanted to run until his lungs burned and his legs went numb.

Eamon.

The familiar awareness of his bound companion returned, just as it had been since the day they sealed their partnership, and he clenched his teeth against a feral howl of joy.

"Eamon," he said and pushed along the thread connecting them. Wherever Eamon was, he wasn't awake, wasn't aware of his surroundings. It was daylight here, but perhaps Eamon was in a different part of the world where it was night.

"My lord," Kiran said again, more alarm in his voice this time. "Are you well? The way you feel..."

"Fine, Kiran. Thank you for your concern." His voice snapped like a whip. He took a deep breath and let it out. "I apologize. It's as if the sea is inside me, and I'm trying not to let it out."

"I don't understand, but if I can help..."

Rafe wondered if it was possible to pass some of the energy to his retainer. If Kiran...

"Feed on me," Rafe said.

Kiran's eyes widened, and his lips parted in a silent gasp. "I'm sorry?"

Rafe gritted his teeth. "Take some of this power from me. It's...it's a lot. I'll open myself to you."

He took Kiran's hands, met his eyes, and relaxed. After a few deep breaths, he was able to lower his guard, open his mind, and let Kiran take some of the burden. It trickled from Rafe to his friend like a lazy summer stream with Rafe keeping a handle on it so it didn't drown him. Kiran's hands clenched on Rafe's, and the other rin's chest heaved as he was filled with more strength than he'd ever had.

"No more," Kiran whispered, cringing away, voice strained.

Rafe broke eye contact, closed himself off to his partner, and held the other rin as he sank to his knees. He'd forgotten how terribly young Kiran was. He'd only stopped needing blood within the past few years and wasn't strong enough to handle a massive influx of energy like Rafe. Or, like Rafe had thought he could, until he did it. Now, he was exhilarated and exhausted, ravenous and overfed.

"I'm sorry," Rafe whispered. "Thank you."

"This is..." Kiran's voice choked off in a gasp, and he struggled for a moment to get himself under control. When he had, he managed to meet Rafe's eyes. "Are you better now?"

"It took the edge off. You should go back, Kiran." The air still shimmered where they'd come through, but the stubborn rin shook his dark head.

"I'm staying with you. I want to help you find Eamon. He's my friend."

Once Eamon woke up, it would be easy to find him. They were in the same world. For now, Rafe decided, it would be best to get out of the sun. He'd lived his whole life in the part of his world where the sun rarely showed itself. This place was the complete opposite.

The quarry stretched out for some distance before reaching the stone walls surrounding them, but a quick spin around showed Rafe the path to climb out. They needed to get moving.

"Come on," he said, helping Kiran up. The shimmering portal had grown smaller, but it was still big enough to fit a body through. He hesitated, debating on shoving Kiran through. It would be bad enough if *he* got stuck in this world, but to have Kiran stuck as well...

"Don't you dare," Kiran whispered, and his hand clenched a fistful of Rafe's cloak. "I'm coming with you."

Despite everything, Rafe smiled. Kiran's devotion was second to none. "You're the best."

"I know," Kiran said, his lips tugging up into a smile too.

As they walked, hoods up to guard against the harsh sunlight, Rafe tried to sort through the knowledge in his mind now. There was a rin in this world, and it was sending ghouls through to Rafe's world. Some of the ghouls arriving there were accidental, he understood from the first ghoul's mind, but some were coming over as...scouts. Scouts for the strange rin. He'd understood the rin was powerful, someone the ghoul understood and...*respected*? Feared. But why did they respect him; why was he sending scouts? All this time Rafe had thought ghouls were mindless monsters.

Even dogs obeyed their masters, he supposed.

He and Kiran traveled to the cave where the ghoul had usually slept and went inside to get out of the sun. The space was large enough to accommodate a large creature, and it smelled of the ghoul's musky, musty flesh.

The desire to rip something limb from limb had edged away after giving some strength to Kiran and expending some while walking, but he was still hyped up. Kiran obviously did, too, as he paced the cave, looking at everything with endless curiosity.

Rafe let out a slow breath before finding the thread connecting him with Eamon and giving it a solid mental pull. He hated to wake his love, but under the circumstances, he guessed Eamon would be forgiving. He focused on Eamon, on the part of his mind that *was* Eamon, and was sure the human had woken. Awareness reached Rafe as it registered in Eamon's mind. Alone. Unfamiliar place. Confused and frightened.

Eamon. Where are you?

Rafe...?

Tell me where you are. I think I can get to you.

...am I dreaming?

No, darling. I'm here. Tell me where you are.

Eamon's relief was so powerful it brought tears to Rafe's eyes.

Beah's village, Eamon responded, which told Rafe exactly nothing. *We had a plan. We were coming home. Tonight, hopefully. But...something happened. I passed out. I...Beah's gone.*

Fear, every bit as powerful as Eamon's relief from a moment ago, slammed down through their bond, and Rafe had to push Eamon's emotions to the back of his mind to keep his own heart from racing in sympathy.

Eamon, relax. Look around. Show me everything you can about where you're at now.

He'd been able to get here with only the ghoul's memories of its home to guide him. Hopefully, now he'd be able to get to Eamon with nothing more than his partner's awareness of his location.

You don't understand. Eamon's mind voice was high and panicky. *They tried to kill him once already. I need to find him.*

Eamon. Rafe tried to soothe his lover.

Eamon bombarded him with thoughts, memories, awareness. He was looking around, out a window into a dusty village. He remembered speaking to a man. A building with cushions on the floor. Guards. A well in a central square. Rafe pieced together a mental image from Eamon's memories.

"I'm not sure how well this is going to go," Rafe said out loud. Kiran came to stand beside him. Eamon's panic was so powerful it was infecting him. It made him anxious and shaky. He did his best to shut it down and concentrate on the location. Only the surroundings, the details around Eamon, not in his mind. As he had at home, he gathered the power in him and clawed across the air.

Nothing happened.

"No!" he groaned.

"Do you need more strength?" Kiran asked. "Take some from me."

Ignoring his retainer, Rafe refocused on Eamon. His immediate sensations, his immediate experiences. Fear, anxiety. Hot air. Stone beneath his bare feet. The woven fabric hanging in the doorway of the room he was in. Leather under his fingers as he put on clothes he didn't recall taking off.

Rafe tried again, and this time, the air shimmered before him. Kiran let out a soft cheer and squeezed his shoulder.

"Let's go get Eamon," Kiran said. Rafe smiled and took his friend's hand, forcing himself forward through the haze of exhaustion creeping up on him.

Chapter Twenty-Two

EAMON

Nothing was going according to plan, so when Rafe and Kiran appeared out of thin air in the small building while Eamon dressed, he almost didn't think to ask how. Almost.

"It's a long story," Rafe said, and then he was pulling Eamon into his arms, and Eamon hugged him with all the strength in his body.

"I missed you," he whispered.

"And I you, my love." Rafe kissed Eamon's hair, squeezing their bodies together, nuzzling his dusty head. They were in a strange place, but at least now they were in a strange place together. The bond between their minds was swimming with emotions. Eamon couldn't tell where his own ended and Rafe's began, but it didn't matter. They were all the same. Relief and love so strong they overflowed from him in the form of tears, and Rafe's trembling breath against his hair told him his stoic lover was just as overwhelmed.

When they managed to part, Eamon grabbed Kiran and pulled him into a hug too. The rin laughed, clapping Eamon on the back.

"It's good to see you, friend." He kissed Eamon's hair, too, much like Rafe had, and Eamon laughed away some of his tears.

"Is everyone else...? I mean, Rose and Lionel and Tuomas... I fell..."

"They're fine," Rafe assured him, and he was dizzy with relief.

The hanging, which closed the room off from the rest of the village, was pulled aside, and a man stood there. His eyes widened when he saw three men standing in the room where only one man should have been lying.

"Who are you?"

Kiran turned to put his back to Eamon's chest, and Rafe stood at his shoulder, forming a solid wall between Eamon and the potential danger. The two of them were both taller than Eamon, and much taller than the guard confronting them now. Eamon pushed between them, unafraid of the sword at the guard's hip.

"Where's my friend?"

"Who are you?" the guard asked the newcomers again, ignoring Eamon completely. "How did you get in there?"

"We walked," Rafe said, surprising Eamon with correct Caddenese.

"I've been here the whole time. You did not walk in there."

Rafe shrugged. "Perhaps you should pay more attention."

"Don't give me attitude!"

Fear for Beah's well-being took away Eamon's patience. His voice lowered into something dangerous, and he asked again, "Where is my friend?"

The guard looked at him, then at his two protectors. After a minute, he said, "Arrested. She's in the priestess's house."

Cold panic and fury bloomed through Eamon's chest. "*He*," he growled. "Take us to him."

"Uh," the guard said and looked at Rafe and Kiran again. "I was told to fetch the medic if you woke up, and…"

"Priestess's house. Now."

"They won't let you in," the guard said, but Eamon was shoving past him.

He'd been afraid when Beah was not at his side when he woke. When he realized he'd been undressed and his weapons were missing, he'd begun to expect the worst. Rafe followed him out of the small house, Kiran on his heels, and Eamon's eyes combed over their surroundings. The priestess lived outside the town, he recalled, and there was only one obvious way out other than the way they'd come in.

"This way?" Eamon asked the startled guard, pointing.

He nodded, mouth hanging open in surprise. "But you can't—"

Rafe grabbed the guard by the front of his robe and spoke in a low, calm voice. "Please. Tell us what we can and cannot do."

"They're preparing a sacrifice. No one's allowed in. It's the law."

"I don't like your law," Rafe said and pushed the guard so he stumbled out of their way but didn't quite fall.

Eamon started in the direction of Alma's house. The villagers were staring from their doorways and windows, gawking at the two hooded strangers now flanking the pale one.

Under his breath, Rafe switched to his native tongue and asked, "Eamon, what is going on?"

As they walked, Eamon summarized the situation. "The village elder and priest are narrow-minded fools, and Beah is queer, so they rigged some lottery to sacrifice him to Shadelin. They feed people to *ghouls*, Rafe."

"What?"

"They *worship* them. They do sacrifices every season or something, choose a person to throw in a pit, and let the ghouls eat. Beah survived, though. He climbed out, and the priestess let him go. He didn't want to return here, but he said the priestess might have the power to travel to other worlds and I...I...pushed him."

Rafe rubbed a comforting hand up and down Eamon's back as they walked. "So he came with you."

"Yeah... He's going to come home with me. I told him he can stay at the manor or in the village or anything he wants. He was living in a cave, Rafe. He saved my life more than once. I don't know. He's just a kid, and he's scared, and I made him..."

He paused for breath. The road out of the far side of the village sloped upward, and he was weak from hunger. It had been hours since their morning meal, and he wasn't sure how long he'd been unconscious.

"We'll get him," Rafe said. "If he saved your life, I owe him. I'll give him anything in my power to give."

They reached a point before long where the trail split. One began to curve down the mountainside, encased in canyon walls on both sides. Safe and easy. The other curved up the mountain, hugging close to the stone on one side and drifting out into oblivion on the other.

"Which way?" Kiran asked.

"Up," Rafe guessed after a second. "I hear voices from up there." He pointed, and far above them, the trail disappeared into a narrow opening.

"Up it is, then."

They had to walk single file, with Eamon in the lead, until they came to the point where the trail turned inward, into another narrow canyon. Guards stood at the entrance of the canyon, and not far beyond them stood a small building—a house. The canyon narrowed to a close, and the house was situated at the end of it like a cork in a bottle.

The guards already had their swords drawn.

"Who are you?" one demanded.

"We're here for the sacrifice," Rafe said before Eamon could speak.

"No one's allowed in," the second guard said. "Six days of cleansing. Not allowed to see anyone."

"Hm," Rafe said.

Eamon turned sideways and pressed himself against the mountain wall, making room for Rafe to squeeze around him. The rin did so, graceful as a cat, and prowled toward the guards. Though he was taller than both of them, they seemed confident in their abilities and didn't back away. Eamon opened his connection to Rafe. Though he'd never seen the rin kill a human—there'd never been cause in the years since Eamon met him—he wondered if Rafe would do it. At home, humans were treated with the utmost respect by rin, as was required by law, but this was not home.

Instead of seeing Rafe's plan to demolish or get around the humans, the connection between them washed Eamon in exhaustion. It was as if Rafe had been running at top speed all day without eating or drinking. He needed rest and energy. If both guards went at him at once with their swords, he might actually be in trouble. What was he thinking?

Before Eamon was able to say a word, both men rushed Rafe. Eamon gasped as Rafe dodged one swing and parried the other, his own sword out of his scabbard in a flash of steel, the slide of metal echoing through the canyon. Night was falling around them, making it difficult to keep track of the movements, but Eamon didn't dare go any closer. Rafe had just enough space inside the entrance of the canyon to maneuver without needing to move close to the edge of the drop off, and Eamon would only be in his way.

The fight didn't last long, but Eamon kept his mind open to Rafe's, and cried out in agony at the slash of a sword across his lover's leg. It had been a calculated risk on Rafe's part, a way to let the guard get close enough, be distracted enough, to let him end things swiftly.

"Let's go," Rafe said once both guards lay on the ground, unconscious. He wasted no time heading toward the small house, but his movements were tense. Kiran caught up and put himself in front of Rafe.

"Feed from me," he said. "Eamon's in no condition, and you're injured."

"This is not the place or time," Rafe whispered, shooting a quick glance to Eamon. "I'm fine."

"You used up all your strength to make those portals. You're weak. Feed from me."

Eamon watched the two, curiosity edging into his concern. Kiran's remark answered the question about where Rafe had been getting his strength in his absence. It answered the question of how Rafe and Kiran had come to this world, but it didn't tell him where Rafe had acquired the ability to create portals. It didn't matter now. If he could do it, he was their escape route. As soon as they got Beah.

"Feed from him," Eamon hissed and went around them. Kiran loved Rafe and always had—it was a powerful love, but a different sort than what Eamon and Rafe shared. Now, though, something had changed. They would need to have a talk once they returned to Seacliff.

"Don't go in there without us." Kiran's voice had a sharp edge.

"I'm just going to look in the window," Eamon returned and pointed at Rafe. "*Feed.* Please."

Rafe sighed but took his retainer's hands. Eamon let them have their moment while he crept ahead to peer in the open window of the hut.

Beah was inside, along with an old woman and Sharim, the holy man who had been in the house with the eldest when Eamon passed out. Beah and the old woman—Alma, if Eamon had to guess—were kneeling with their hands bound in their laps. Both wore simple shifts. Alma's long gray hair hung loose around her bowed head, and her wrinkled brown skin sagged loose off a thin frame.

Light from a fire in the hearth and candles around the room illuminated the expression of fear and fury on Beah's face. He looked so vulnerable, arms bare and legs exposed from mid-thigh to feet. Shadows played across his face, but Eamon was certain the young man had a bruise across his cheek. Anger swelled up in Eamon's chest at the thought of them hurting his friend, and he turned his gaze away from Beah's face to stop himself from launching into the room and throttling the holy man who now stood with his back to the window.

Sharim was speaking in a calm, even cadence, and it only took Eamon a moment of listening to realize he was reciting the rites of the twelve paths. He was on the Rite of Compassion now. The bastard had no right...

A soft noise from behind Eamon drew his attention, and he turned as Kiran sank to his knees and rested his forehead against Rafe's hip. Even in his anger, the sight filled him with warmth and tenderness. He liked Kiran, and he guessed Kiran was pleased at the opportunity to serve Rafe in such a vital way. Eamon returned to them, as quietly as possible, and knelt beside Kiran to embrace him.

"Thank you for taking care of him," he said.

Kiran chuckled softly and stroked Eamon's arm. "He's taken care of me for how long now? I'm glad to return the favor."

Rafe patted both their heads. "Get up, boys. We're in the middle of something. You can cuddle later."

Eamon squeezed his friend, then helped him up and recounted what he'd seen in the hut.

"No weapons?" Rafe asked with a nod.

"I didn't see any."

Rafe set off toward the hut without another word, striding more confidently after feeding. Eamon and Kiran kept on his heels.

When he reached the doorway, Rafe didn't hesitate, but tore the hanging down in one sharp movement, startling Sharim into silence.

"Who are you?" the holy man boomed after the instant of surprise had passed.

"A friend," Rafe said, then paused and pointed past Sharim at Beah. "Of his."

"You are interrupting the cleansing rituals! The gods will not forgive you."

"You and I worship different gods, priest." Rafe stepped into the hut, but Sharim put himself in front of the prisoners.

"Shadelin, god of death and fear and sleepless nights, protect us from this heretic!"

Once Rafe had moved far enough into the hut, Eamon squeezed in behind him and went around his side.

"Eamon!" Beah cried and relief shone in tears pooling in his dark eyes. He did indeed have a bruise on his cheek, and a cut on his lip, and Eamon took a deep breath to control his anger.

"*You!*" Sharim shouted. The book in his hand snapped shut with a sharp thud. "Stay away from the sacrifices!"

"You're sacrificing your own priestess?"

"She has not served the gods as she should. She allowed this one—" He pointed an accusatory finger at Beah. "—to go free. We have had three children die this season already. The gods are not pleased with her."

"The morroul are animals!" Alma shouted. "You are a fool to feed them!"

"Heretic!" Sharim screeched. "Heretic! The gods—"

"Enough," Rafe said, grabbing Sharim's arm to pull him aside.

The holy man started whaling on Rafe with his holy book. He got in a few solid strikes, bloodying Rafe's lip before the rin caught his wrist to restrain him. Rather than look angry or pained, Rafe's expression spoke of a mildly irritated parent restraining their flailing toddler. The holy man and his holy book were like an insect to him.

Eamon took advantage of Sharim's inability to move and stepped away from the side wall to kneel in front of Beah.

"I'm glad you're all right," Beah said, his voice barely more than a whisper. Eamon smiled and began working the knots in his bindings loose.

"Yeah, I'm all right. So are you, now. We're going home."

He got the knots untied and freed Beah's wrists, and the young man threw his arms around Eamon. Surprised by the show of affection from his somewhat distant new friend, Eamon nevertheless smiled and returned it, squeezing Beah and planting a quick kiss on his temple.

"Here," he said when Beah leaned back. He swung his cloak off his shoulders and wrapped it around his friend, giving him some modesty over his thin shift dress.

"Thank you."

Sharim continued squawking in the background as Eamon untied the priestess, Alma. She watched him suspiciously the whole time but didn't speak.

"Let's go," Eamon said once she was free.

Beah was on his trail in an instant, but Alma did not follow. Instead, she grabbed something off a table near the wall, and before Eamon registered what it was, she lunged at Sharim and Rafe, shrieking.

"The gods help those who help themselves! *I* keep this village safe!"

"Whoa!" Rafe cried, and let go of Sharim with one hand to catch at Alma.

Eamon saw what she had grabbed then: a dagger. The blade glinted in the firelight, and he recognized it as his own weapon, no doubt taken from him when he passed out earlier. A swear tore out of him as Rafe managed to grab her dagger-wielding hand while still holding Sharim's book-wielding hand.

"Come on," Kiran said, holding out a hand to Beah and Eamon. They both edged closer to him but didn't leave the hut.

Sharim and Alma were clawing at each other. Rafe couldn't hold them far enough apart to prevent them from doing any damage. Instead, he twisted both their wrists, digging fingers into tendons to force them to drop their respective weapons. The book landed with a flutter of pages and a thud. The dagger *fwumped* onto the dirt floor and went no further. Rafe's prisoners cried out and struggled, their focus turned to him instead of each other.

"STOP." His voice boomed, and Eamon's breath caught. Even directed at others, Rafe's commanding voice sent a chill along his skin as heat rushed straight to his groin.

And Sharim and Alma stopped.

Rafe shoved them both back, away from each other, and bent lightning quick to pick up the dagger. Sharim fell on his ass, but Alma only stumbled, surprisingly spry for a woman her age. Rafe offered the dagger, hilt-first, to the side without taking his eyes off the two people before him, without even looking to make sure anyone was there to accept it. He didn't need to look. He knew exactly where his lover was, and Eamon stepped forward and took the hilt. He hadn't spotted his bow anywhere in the room, but the familiar dagger comforted him.

"Woman," Rafe said, voice still deep and authoritative. She glared at him. "Are you able to travel between worlds?"

Her face took on an uncertain expression. "No."

"Liar," Beah snapped. All eyes turned to him, but he was glaring at Alma. "I saw you make morroul disappear."

She shook her head. "That is not travel between worlds."

"Yes, it is," Rafe cut in. "I saw their memories. They start out here and end up in my world. You have gatekeeper abilities."

She looked confused and angry, but before she was able to respond, Sharim stepped forward.

"What is this about? What have you been doing, woman? Have you done harm to the gods' creatures?"

"They are animals," Alma returned, glaring. "Nothing more."

"You can create portals," Rafe said, loudly enough to drown out Sharim's protests. "You can, and you will. We will not stay here."

She shook her head, and Eamon realized the expression he'd thought was confusion, was actually fear. She was scared to create a portal. To travel between worlds. Why? Surely it wasn't religious convictions—she was already disobeying the gods by killing their ghouls, wasn't she? But Beah had made it clear that travel between worlds and travel outside the village were forbidden. Eamon's heart raced. She'd been his only hope. They had to get through to her, get her to send them home. But...Rafe had made it here without her. If he'd done it once, maybe...

Kiran, who'd stepped outside to keep watch, called through the doorway with poorly veiled panic in his voice. "We've developed a problem."

As he scrambled into the hut, a sound reached them. A scuffling, snuffling, animal sound echoing from the canyon beyond the hut.

A ghoul.

Chapter Twenty-Three

RAFE

"Now might be a good time to use your new magic, my lord," Kiran said.

Rafe stepped to the window, keeping against the wall, and peered carefully out toward the source of the sound...

Just in time to see a second ghoul materialize out of shimmering air.

The first one was a dog-like creature, shaggy and brown, with a broad chest and wide head. It stood midway between them and the canyon's opening, snuffling around the area where Rafe had fed from Kiran only moments ago. The second arrival was more reptilian, with scales and split-toed feet akin to hands. It turned and went to the entrance of the canyon, where the bodies of the men Rafe had disabled lay. He turned away as its long mouth opened to reveal jagged teeth-like protrusions.

"What new magic?" Eamon asked finally.

Rafe had already tried to summon up the strength it took to open a portal, but it seemed he'd lost it. It had taken an immense expenditure to open the previous portals, and the exhaustion had led to an injury. What he'd recently taken from Kiran was keeping him going, healing the sword wound and giving him the strength to appear normal, but he wanted—*needed*—rest and a deep, slow, intimate feeding like he hadn't had since the night before Eamon disappeared. There was no time for it now.

"I drained a ghoul," Rafe admitted. "It gave me the ability to create portals, but unfortunately it seems it was temporary."

"You fed from a ghoul?" Eamon said, incredulous.

"And read another's mind," Kiran chimed in.

Rafe gave him a scathing look. "Not helping."

"Sorry, my lord."

To his lover, Rafe said, "Yes, Eamon. I found one that was able to travel the worlds, and I drained it. Taking its life evidently gave me its abilities. But, as I said, temporarily."

Sharim, who'd fallen silent at the sound of the ghouls feasting outside, suddenly found his voice. "This is your fault." He was looking at Alma. "The morroul *never* come this close. They're punishing us! They require a sacrifice!"

"Shut your mouth, or I'll sacrifice you!" Rafe snapped, glaring. The holy man was tiresome, to say the least, and Rafe didn't have time or energy to exert on a squawking fool. At least one of the ghouls out there had the ability to create portals. Which meant if he was able to get it isolated, worn down, and pinned, he'd be able to feed on it and regain the ability. Hopefully.

How many good soldiers had it taken to accomplish that with the last one? All he had now was Kiran and four humans, one of whom was unlikely to help and the other elderly. He peered around the window frame again. Both ghouls were digging into the guards. It was a shame, but at least they were unconscious for it.

"I need one alive, but I can't do it by myself. I am open to suggestions," he said to the small group gathered around him. Eamon was tapping his dagger blade against his thigh, lip caught between his teeth, and even now with potential death so close, Rafe was filled with the desire to take Eamon's lip between his own teeth, run his hand along his thigh... Gods, what he would give to be home in bed with him right now.

"Is there another way out?" Eamon asked, looking to Alma. When she shook her head, he spun to Sharim. "Would the villagers help us?"

Sharim scoffed. "They are here for the women." He waved a hand in Beah and Alma's direction. "Simply hand them over, and the gods—"

"They are here for *anything they can eat*," Eamon returned. "Maybe we'll hand *you* over."

The robed man paled. "They are not here for me."

"How do you explain them munching the guards out there? They're not here for *them* either!"

While Sharim tried to babble an explanation, Rafe peered out the window again. The canyon was narrow, and the hut built into the end of it. It was a straight shot down a ghoul's throat if they went out the front door, but there was no back way out.

"I'll go ask for help."

All attention shifted to the small, soft-featured man wearing Eamon's cloak. Beah.

Sharim laughed. "You?"

"Me."

"Beah..." Eamon looked to Rafe and Kiran, brows knitted. No one was objecting to Beah's proposal. After a moment, he continued, "Will the villagers be willing to attack the morroul?"

Beah's lips pressed together in a thoughtful line. "I'll figure something out."

Rafe nodded, then tensed. The sounds of flesh ripping and bones breaking had fallen silent. Everything had fallen silent.

"Get back," Rafe said suddenly, grabbing Eamon and Kiran and pushing them toward the far wall. *"Get back!"*

They moved with him, Sharim scrambling to follow, and hit the wall just as a large, furry arm reached through the door and clawed at them. Rafe and Kiran drew their swords and slashed at it, and the ghoul let out a shriek and withdrew.

"You cannot kill a servant of the gods!" Sharim cried, but he was pressed against the rear of the hut in fear the same as everyone else.

No matter what religious beliefs one held, the idea of being eaten alive never appealed when the possibility was staring one in the face. It was easy to ignore the reality of it from the comfort of a house of prayer when the closest you got to the real carnage was watching a villager choose a lottery tile. Reality was uglier. But Rafe wasn't there to lecture this priest on his poor leadership abilities.

Sharim dropped to his knees and began praying. Rafe positioned himself between Alma and Beah and the door, while Kiran stood between Sharim and Eamon and the door.

The second swipe came from the lizard-like ghoul, and Rafe had a second to wonder if the thing's limbs would grow back upon removal before he tested the theory with a strong downward swing. Flesh and bone parted under the vicious attack, and the ghoul hissed as it withdrew a bleeding stump. Its severed leg flopped to the floor, oozing thick, black liquid.

The furry ghoul, sensing weakness, attacked its companion. Hellacious snarls and hisses reached them. The hut shook as two large bodies wrestled on the stone outside and slammed each other against canyon walls.

Rafe swore. He knew for certain one of those ghouls had the ability to create portals. He didn't want them to kill each other and rob him of a magic source.

He looked toward Beah. "How fast can you run, boy?"

"Fast."

"Good."

Rafe glanced at Eamon. He stood with his back to the wall, knuckles white as he gripped the dagger. With another muttered curse, Rafe crossed the room to his lover and pressed a kiss against his lips, delving into his mouth to taste him. He kept his sword to the side and brought his free hand up to cup Eamon's cheek, enjoying the coarse brush of whiskers against his palm. The warmth of his lover's body tempted him, promised delights and pleasures he could only imagine right now. He drew away, breathless.

"I'm going to get you out of here," he said. "Kiran, with me. Beah, get ready to run."

Chapter Twenty-Four

BEAH

"No!" Eamon protested, but the man with very dark skin—Kiran—put a hand on Eamon's chest as he tried to go after his husband.

Beah didn't understand the dark man's language, and he didn't have time to watch what happened next. He followed Rafe out the door, barefoot, huddled in Eamon's cloak. He only hoped he'd be able to convince someone to come help.

Outside the shelter of the small hut, his legs stopped moving. The creatures were huge. Even in the darkness, their shapes loomed above him like something from a nightmare. They fought nearby, rearing up and scuffling at each other with claws and teeth. The metallic stink of blood made Beah's nose wrinkle.

"If they come after you, I will distract them," Rafe said in a low voice. "Keep running. Do not stop."

Kiran exited the hut behind Beah, with Eamon on his heels. Rafe spat a word Beah guessed was a curse followed by Eamon's name and something in a commanding tone. Eamon scoffed and shifted his grip on the dagger in his hand. Beah didn't need to understand their language to know Rafe was trying to get Eamon to stay inside. He didn't need to understand their language to know Eamon wasn't going to obey. Eamon was clearly terrified, but his shoulders were squared and jaw clenched. It gave Beah strength. If Eamon, with his many fears, could face these monsters, so could Beah.

Rafe sighed and muttered something, giving in. With a gesture to Beah, Rafe walked toward the open end of the canyon, and Beah followed. The creatures were focused on each other. Beah looked to the star-studded sky beyond Rafe's shoulder, refusing to give the creatures his attention. The sounds of their scuffle continued in his right ear, and he moved without pausing, until the sounds changed.

"*Run!*" Rafe yelled, and Beah didn't pause to look back. He dodged around the tall man's side and bolted, holding Eamon's too-large cloak up like a dress, doing his best to ignore the weight of his unbound chest and forcing himself not to cry out as small stones cut into his feet and the creatures roared behind him in what he hoped was pain at a sword thrust.

There was nothing but for Beah to keep running and send up a prayer that his new friends would survive. They were from Wesige's world, the huntress, one of the earliest paths in life. If the gods were real, surely they wouldn't let these strangers die here, on Shadelin's world, and deprive them of eight more lives.

But then, the gods *weren't* real, were they? Beah had been able to leave the village, which the gods supposedly forbade. Beah had survived the sacrifice and seen Alma send morroul to another world instead of honoring them as they were meant to be honored. If she was to be believed, she'd done this with dozens of sacrifices, and the gods had not struck her down.

There were no gods, and they were on their own, just as likely to die here and now as in their own world.

Beah put everything into his legs and sprinted down the length of the canyon and through the bloodbath of Len and Calan's remains, the two who had been posted as guards at the top of the narrow path. He tried to think of a likely story to convince the villagers to help him. Maybe if he didn't tell them the morroul were the danger... Once they got to the canyon, they'd be forced to defend themselves regardless of where the threat came from... Would it be wrong for him to put them in such peril?

Shit, they'd made him fast for days, cut his hands, and put him in a pit deeper than he was tall so the monsters would come eat him. Did he really give a damn about endangering them?

He moved as fast as he was able on the narrow path hugging the cliff. In the dark, one wrong step might kill him, but he shuffled along with a hand on the stone beside him as a guide. His heart pounded in his throat, and he gasped in breaths. He knew very well when he returned to the top of the cliff, there was a good chance his companions would be dead. Or perhaps, they would come out victorious, get what they needed, and leave without him.

No. He shoved the thought aside immediately. Eamon wouldn't leave without him. Not after everything they'd gone through.

When Beah hit solid ground again, he started running...and then stopped as sounds reached him through the roar of blood pounding in his ears. High sounds. Panicked sounds. People screaming.

People screaming in the village.

Firelight flickered in the distance, around the bend leading to the outskirts of the village. He took off again, running in the direction of the only place he'd ever called home. Rock scraped his bare feet, pieces of stone jabbing into the sensitive arches, but he kept going, Eamon's borrowed cloak flapping about him. Only when he came around the bend and the village spread out before him did he stop and stare in horror.

Huge creatures bounded around the houses. More than he could count in the darkness. Torches and oil lamps burned in the only street. Some had been knocked over. Fire licked up the woven door hanging of a nearby house, and inside, people were screaming.

His feet wouldn't carry him any farther. One ghoul, he would face. Two ghouls, distracted by their potential murderers, he might slip by. But more?

The screams came from everywhere. Inside homes. Inside the holy building. The streets. The garden. In the uncertain light, the scene before him played out like a nest of ants with water dumped on them. He saw nothing but writhing, flailing, panicked movement, people and monsters rushing about with urgency and, in the morrouls' case, glee. It was like the harvest banquet—dozens of dishes laid out before them. Except the dishes were the people who'd helped raise Beah, played with him growing up, come to his mother for ointments and cures...

They were the people who had watched as he drew the "lucky" tile. Had watched as he was stripped of his belongings, paraded to the village center, and cleansed. Had assured him they were proud of him, that he was fortunate to be chosen to join the gods and spend an eternity at their sides.

Now, who was being chosen to join the gods?

He watched the madness for an eternity, but he didn't actually see it. His mind refused to comprehend the events before him. He couldn't remember why he was there, what he was supposed to do. All he wanted was to run away.

Run. *Run.*

Rafe and the others, at the top of the path. They needed help. There was clearly no one here to help them. Beah might find a sword, perhaps. He doubted his skills with a blade would be helpful. A bow and arrows might help Eamon, but...again, what difference would it truly make? They needed more bodies.

Beah took a deep breath and pushed away the panic. There had to be something else, a way to...to make the morroul less dangerous. Poison. Sedatives. Something.

He remembered the herbalist who'd visited the village years ago, and his heart leapt into his throat.

He had to get to his mother.

A narrow side path ran behind the houses, looping the village to alleviate travel in the village center. He moved to the path, keeping low until he'd put himself in the shelter of the first building. He let out a relieved breath once he had a solid division between himself and the mayhem of the village. In that manner, he managed to make it around to the sixth house, the one he'd grown up in.

One of the morroul let out a horrible roar, and Beah leaned around the side of the structure in an attempt to see what was happening. He didn't have a good vantage point, and he had to sidle around the edge and crouch near the front corner, between his mother's home and the neighbor's, Kara, who made the lovely woven baskets he'd always coveted.

Some of the villagers had armed themselves and were fighting a lanky, black-skinned morroul. The thing moved like a reed on the wind, doing agile flips and twists to avoid their swords. In the darkness, it was impossible to tell for certain who the brave defenders were, but they weren't long for this world. The morroul caught one of the men in a long-fingered hand and bit into his shoulder. Beah flinched and looked away as the man shrieked in pain.

Smoke from the burning hangings clouded the air. Beah did his best to block all his senses, to ignore the screams and the roars, the smell of smoke, the pain in his feet. So far, he hadn't been seen. He hoped his luck would continue. With a deep, slow breath, he steadied his nerves and darted around the corner of the building, onto the main path, and then, quick as a flash, he pushed aside the door hanging and dove into his mother's home.

She screamed.

He screamed.

Then she saw his face and gasped. Said his old name. He didn't bother correcting her.

"Mother, do you remember the herbalist who came to the village several summers ago?"

She stared at him without answering, and he moved closer and grabbed her shoulders.

"Mother!"

Her eyes were too wide, breath coming in short, rapid gasps. When she was finally able to speak, she asked, "Aren't you supposed to be with the priestess?"

"Since when do I do what I'm supposed to? Do you remember the herbalist, or not?"

"The gods are furious. You deprived them of their sacrifice and—"

Beah spat to the side and let go of his mother. "They're hungry animals, nothing more."

He got up. The door hanging and open windows did nothing to muffle the screams from outside, but he tried to block them out. Eamon. His friend, the man he'd saved and who had saved him. He had a way out, one that didn't involve dying or living alone for the rest of his life. All he had to do was get back up the mountain and help them.

He went to the cabinet where his mother kept her herbs.

She watched him from her crouched position on the floor. Strands of graying hair hung loose over her face. Combined with her crazed eyes and hunched shoulders, it made her look savage and dangerous. Beah tried to push the imagery from his head. She was his mother, and she was the village medic. Savage and dangerous were the last two words he'd think to use for her normally.

"What are you doing?" she whispered. She crawled toward him and grabbed a fistful of his cloak to try to pull him to the floor. He jerked the thick cloth out of her hand. "They'll see you!"

"They're a little busy right now, Mother," he said, dropping vials into the pouch-like sleeves of the cloak he wore.

"What are you doing?" she asked again.

"I need these. I'll return what I don't use." Not like she'd have much use for this stuff with the way things were going.

As soon as the thought crossed his mind, he scolded himself. Family came first, right? The village was his family. They'd always been... They'd helped raise him. Taught him how to sow seeds, how to care for wounds, how to dress... *You're just a foolish, broken girl. Your own father left because he couldn't stand the idea of raising you.*

It was just one of many things said to him here. Hateful things. Hurtful things. The unexpected memory of them froze him in place, fist clenching into a ball around the clay jar in his hand. Fuck his family. No one had defended him. No one. He threw the last few jars into his borrowed cloak and turned toward the door.

"Wait!" His mother's hand grasped a fistful of his cloak again. "You're not going out there, are you?"

"Yes."

"You'll die!"

"Isn't that what you want?" He jerked the cloak out of her hand again, turned, and flung aside the hanging without looking back.

Chapter Twenty-Five

EAMON

As soon as Beah was out of sight, Kiran began urging Eamon toward the house. Rafe was on the other side of the two ghouls, his back to the entrance of the canyon, with their attention on him.

Eamon resisted Kiran's hand. "He'll die!"

"Just *go inside*, Eamon! I'll help him!"

As much as Eamon hated it, he was useless with his inferior human speed and strength. It didn't make much difference whether he was inside or out, but he took a step toward the shelter, and then another, so Kiran would go help Rafe. Satisfied with Eamon's obedience, Kiran finally left.

Eamon stopped retreating. He watched in the starlit darkness as Kiran threw himself into the fight, attacking one of the ghouls from behind. It spun around in fury, but he'd gotten in a solid attack on its inner leg, and it buckled under the weight, giving him time to dart out of reach.

It was difficult to keep track of the fight visually, with two large figures fighting two small figures in a narrow space in the dark, but Eamon was able to keep in touch with Rafe through their bond. He was hurt, but not fatally. The wound would heal in an instant if he was able to feed on one of the ghouls. He was mostly playing with them, distracting them, but it was wearing him down. What little energy he'd drawn from Kiran to heal the wound sustained from fighting the humans was running out.

How long had Beah been gone? Had anything happened to him? The villagers were by no means on his side, but perhaps if he was able to convince them Sharim was in danger, they would help. Damn it, Eamon should have gone with him.

Pain lanced through his body, and he cried out and staggered. It took a split second for him to register it wasn't his own pain and force himself to ignore it. Then, he was able to focus on the fight before him and see one of the two smaller shadows tumble across the ground to lie motionless some distance away.

"Rafe!"

Not dead. If he was dead, Eamon wouldn't be alive.

He moved before thought or reason could stop him, sprinting through the canyon toward the creatures.

No, Eamon!

There was no chance he was going to listen.

Before he covered even half the distance to the ghouls, though, the charging dog-like ghoul roared and reared, spinning on its hind legs away from Rafe. Eamon froze. The lizard ghoul let out a shriek and writhed toward Eamon and Kiran and the priestess's hut.

It's Beah! Rafe said into his mind, and Eamon ran to Kiran and pulled him by the arm to the hut. The ghouls were distracted, screaming, moving away from the front of the canyon—away from Rafe. Their large bodies made it impossible for Eamon and Kiran to do anything but retreat into the hut.

Sharim was praying again. Alma lay on the floor, unconscious or...worse.

"What did you *do*?" Eamon screamed, but Sharim was busy with his recitations and didn't stop to answer.

Kiran knelt by the woman and held a hand in front of her mouth.

"She's alive."

Outside, the ghouls were howling by the front door of the hut, the awful noises so loud they shook the walls, vibrating in Eamon's ears and making his teeth chatter. Their bodies loomed outside the window, dark fur sliding past the open space, white scales shimmering in its wake as they circled and paced.

What's happening? Eamon opened himself to Rafe. The pain resurfaced in his mind, and he groaned. His stomach.

But now Beah was there, kneeling beside Rafe, asking, *What can I do to help*?

"He needs to feed," Eamon muttered.

From his place by the front window, Kiran swore. "We can't get to him. What did Beah do?"

"I don't know," Eamon answered.

The ghouls continued their pacing just outside the hut, snarling at each other and likely at Rafe and Beah, but they weren't trying to go near them. They weren't trying to get to those inside the hut either. But it didn't mean they wouldn't eat them the second they stepped out the door.

Rafe, what do we do? Eamon's fear instincts were set off at the large animals pacing just outside the door, and the dagger in his hand shook. He needed to get to his lover and Beah. He needed this to be done with, so he could collapse and shake and let out the panic bubbling just under the surface.

Beah is coming to you.

How? Even in his head, Eamon's voice went too high.

Shh, my love. You've made yourself a clever friend there. He'll get you out.

What about you?

I'm not going anywhere.

But the ghouls—

The ghouls began snarling and yowling, claws scrabbling on stone, and Eamon stepped away from the door. His back bumped into Kiran's chest, and the rin stepped in front of him and drew his sword.

The hanging swung open, and Beah ducked in. He had a strip of his shift torn off and wrapped around his nose and mouth.

"Come with me," he said and stepped aside, holding the hanging open for them to follow. Eamon and Kiran stared at him in silent shock. "Come *on*. The smell won't last forever."

"What sm—" As Eamon began to ask, a scent reached him through the window. It burned his eyes and nose like inhaling crushed pepper, and his eyes filled with tears. Behind him, Sharim began to cough but kept trying to recite his rituals. His coughs drew Beah's attention, and he saw Alma.

"Can you carry her?" Beah asked, eyes on Kiran.

Kiran glanced at Eamon, who translated. And then, the rin, one hand over his nose and mouth, nodded and took a step toward her. Sharim started to protest, and Eamon spun around, dagger tip aimed at the holy man.

"I am not a violent man, Sharim, but by the gods you are pushing me. We're taking this woman and this man, and we are going."

Sharim subsided and let Kiran sheathe his sword and pick up the elderly woman from the floor. Eamon wasn't sure what he'd discover when he stepped out the door, but even if he'd made a guess, he would have been wrong.

The ghouls were both pressed up against the canyon wall to the right of the door, hissing and cowering away from...smoke. It seemed to rise from the ground around them, pinning them to the wall. They didn't even attempt to lash out as the group slipped out the door and ran past them.

"What are they doing?" Eamon asked.

"Remember the herbalist I told you about?" Beah said over his shoulder. "The one the villagers chased out when she tried to teach ways to fend off the morroul?"

"Yes?"

"Before they chased her off, she taught me and my mother. It's a mixture of herbs that repels them. They hate the smell."

"I can sympathize," Eamon muttered. He translated quickly for Kiran.

"Wasn't he supposed to be getting help?" Kiran asked. "Getting other villagers to help?"

To Beah, Eamon said, "Did the villagers refuse to help?"

Beah said nothing and was saved from the need to answer when they reached Rafe. A torch lay at his side, casting a flickering orange glow over him. Eamon fell to his knees beside his lover, dropping his dagger carelessly to the side to cup Rafe's cheeks in his hands. The front of Rafe's tunic was black, his hand pressed to his belly stained a similar shiny black, and his face pale in the dark.

"We're getting you out of here," Eamon said. "Tell me what to do."

"He needs to feed," Kiran said, lowering his unconscious burden to the ground and kneel at Rafe's other side.

"I need to feed on the ghoul," Rafe clarified. His voice was strained, but he smiled. "Help me up. Get me over there. Beah has them pinned with his stinky powder."

Eamon and Kiran looped Rafe's arms over their shoulders and helped him up, ignoring his tension and gasps of pain. Beah led the way, holding the torch in one hand and a bundle of fabric in the other. The ghouls were pinned so close to the canyon wall they couldn't—or at least, wouldn't—dare move past each other. It was a shock they weren't attacking each other. The lizard-like one currently faced them, and Beah led the way toward its head.

"It's weakened. I just need eye contact," Rafe said, his voice strained.

They moved closer, shuffling, cautious. Eamon felt the instant Rafe connected with the thing. The ghoul went rigid, fighting the intrusion, but once Rafe had gotten in deep enough, it relaxed. It walked toward them, ignoring the smoking bundles, and Kiran's weight shifted, readying to run if necessary. Beah moved to the side, avoiding the monster, taking slow, careful steps. Its paws were as large as Eamon's entire torso, claws like his forearms, dark eyes as big as his fists. He didn't move, no matter how much he wanted to flee. Between the fear and the smoke, breathing was a challenge, but he held his ground, supporting Rafe until the thing lay down in front of them, still under Rafe's spell, and he took most of his own weight back. Rafe lifted his arms off his supporters' shoulders to step forward and lay hands on the monster's face.

Eamon's vision blurred as the thing's life flowed into Rafe, knitting his torn belly and chest, and then filling him, surging into him like a river breaking through a dam, dizzying, overpowering. Kiran stood close by, hand on his hilt, ready to defend, but the need did not arise. Peaceful as a summer breeze, the ghoul's breath left its lungs, and it did not inhale again.

And Eamon collapsed.

Chapter Twenty-Six

RAFE

"I've got him," Kiran said, catching Eamon before he hit the ground.

"This happened before," Beah said, seeing the concern on Rafe's face. "In the holy house."

"We can take care of him at home," Kiran said. "Can you make portals from that ghoul?"

Rafe shook his head, eyes not leaving his lover's sagging form. He was healed, and the ghoul's power bolstered his strength, left him overwhelmed by the vicious, animalistic need to fight, fuck, eat, kill. He would have to take from the second ghoul, the lizard one. It lay against the canyon wall, hissing with each shallow breath. Rafe walked around the still form of the first ghoul, coming close again to the hut.

Sharim stood at the door, a horrified expression on his face, and Rafe made a detour. As the distance between him and Sharim lessened, the holy man seemed to shrink.

"Try to interfere," Rafe whispered, bracing a hand on either side of the doorway. "Just try. I dare you."

"I need not interfere," Sharim returned in a shaky voice, "for the gods see all, and judge those who must be judged."

"Indeed they do, Sharim." Unable to resist, Rafe gave the man a little shove. In his power-heightened state, a little shove knocked the man backward onto his ass.

The second ghoul was easy to overcome thanks to Rafe's newly drawn strength, and it gave up its powers and its memories with only a pathetic attempt at a fight. He saw the moment it had caught his scent, the tang of rin blood from a startling distance. It had come here because of him, not out of any godly missive. Rafe then got more images of the mysterious figure giving orders. He gained memories of this ghoul sneaking through other worlds—unfamiliar places—and then returning to its master.

Scouts. For what purpose?

The ghoul didn't understand its goal. It was merely a tool. And, like a tool, Rafe repurposed it to suit his needs. He drained it, took everything down to the last spark of its life, and when he thought of home and lifted his hand, the magic was there waiting to be used.

He thought about the courtyard first, to make a grand entrance and show off his new powers... Then he reconsidered and focused on his chambers: the stone hearth and polished dark wood floors, plush carpets in earthy tones and white drapes hanging over ceiling-to-floor windows. When he pushed, the magic let him sink his fingers through the world and rip open a space big enough for them to pass through. He took Eamon from Kiran and sent his retainer back for the unconscious woman.

"After you," he said, gesturing Beah through first. The young man hesitated, staring at the shimmering air in wonder and fear. Then, with a deep breath, he stepped through. Rafe waited for Kiran to go before him and then followed on their heels.

The world went liquid and shimmered around them, the rush of magic like a lover's caress over his cheeks and exposed arms, and then they were in his chambers.

Beah stood awestruck, turning in a slow circle on the gray stone floor of Rafe's main room. Kiran laid Alma on a sofa near the hearth and then dropped into a chair near her. His body slouched heavily with exhaustion, and Rafe sympathized. Exhaustion plagued him even as power coursed through his body like fire. If Eamon had been well, Rafe didn't think he'd have been able to restrain his urges. But Eamon wasn't well.

Rafe laid his lover out on the bed and looked down at his familiar, comforting face. He was dirty and scruffy, but he was where he belonged now. It wasn't right though. He was still and silent, breathing, but nothing more. Rafe needed his smile, his laughter. The thought that all this might have been for naught—to go to another world and fight and kill only to bring his lover home and have him die—filled Rafe with so much anger he wanted to scream.

Breathe, he reminded himself. Usually, that thought was aimed at Eamon as he trembled in the grip of fear. *Just breathe. There is nothing else right now. Just breathe.*

A sound like footsteps behind him drew his attention before a somewhat-familiar voice spoke.

"This is an interesting development."

Rafe spun around. From near the bed, Kiran sprang to his feet, and Beah turned to regard the speaker.

The rin was tall, pale as snow, with eyes the color of a summer sky and hair like a raven's feather. He wore black leather from toe to hip and an ornately embroidered doublet covered his lean torso. A small entourage emerged from the shimmering air behind him—two rin, one as tall and pale as he was, the other slightly shorter and slightly darker, followed by a dark-skinned human. The air stopped shimmering behind her, and Rafe assumed she was a gatekeeper.

"What have you gotten yourself into, Lord Rafe of Seacliff Manor?"

By the time the surprise passed and recognition set in, Rafe had been staring long enough to be considered rude. But he didn't kneel. There was power flowing through him, two ghouls' worth of power, and the two people he loved most were in this room with him. This near stranger, by merely entering the room and speaking a few words, was challenging him.

"I don't believe I was informed of your visit, my king," Rafe said, taking the steps down from his bedroom to the main room.

Kiran stood motionless, taking his cues from his lord but tense and afraid. Beah didn't understand the language and stood with a confused expression.

"I did not make an advance announcement," King Soren said. The words were unhurried as he looked Rafe over from head to toe. "Where *did* you get all that delicious power? I sensed you the instant you returned to this world."

"Ghouls," Rafe said and shrugged. "Two of them."

"Hm." Soren advanced, closing the distance between them, eyes intent only on the lord of the manor and not his stunned retainer or confused off-world companion. "Do you have a death wish, Lord Rafe?"

Rafe's resolve shivered. Was he being threatened? "No, my king."

"Why, then, would you feed on ghouls?"

"It's an awfully long story."

"Never mind, then," Soren said. "I have no patience for prattle."

Quick as lightning, his hands were on both sides of Rafe's face. Their eyes met, and he was controlling Rafe's head just as Rafe had controlled the ghouls when he dove into their minds. The king burrowed into his mind, sifting through his memories, and Rafe had to force away the urge to fight it. Even if he did fight, he doubted he'd have come out victorious. The king hadn't become the king by being weak.

"I see," Soren said, withdrawing. His hands on Rafe's head kept him upright as his knees went liquid in the wake of the mind invasion. "And this is your bound companion?" He let go of Rafe, and the rin managed to keep his feet and turn to watch Soren walk up to the bed where Eamon lay.

"Eamon, Your Majesty," Rafe said, swallowing against dizziness and panic and anger. "Yes."

"And the humans from the other world?" His attention turned to the room at large, and he spotted Beah. "Ah. The boy."

When Soren approached, Beah edged away, wide-eyed and looking to Rafe for help.

"He only speaks Caddenese," Rafe said. The poor boy didn't know who Soren was. Given everything he'd just experienced and witnessed, he was right to be scared and suspicious.

"How inconvenient." Soren smiled at Beah, bowed at the waist, and offered his hand. Again, Beah turned his attention to Rafe, who nodded, before accepting the gesture. As Soren straightened, he caught Beah's eye, and the young man went stiff with tension. Then, just as quickly, he sagged, and Soren lowered him gently to the floor. "He has a head full of interesting information. I wonder about the old lady."

He straightened and turned to the sofa where Alma lay, a calculating expression in his eyes.

Rafe's attention remained on Beah. The boy sat, stunned, with his back to the wall, blinking as if he'd just emerged from underground into daylight.

"What did you do to him?"

"Gave him knowledge," the king said. "Learning another language is such a time-consuming endeavor. This will save him some struggle."

Beah's eyes had gone unfocused at the exchange, and Rafe turned to Soren in shock. The rin had planted an entire language in Beah's head in the blink of an eye. Rafe swallowed at the implications of such skill, and as Soren took steps toward the hearth, Rafe turned to keep him in sight. Doing so meant turning away from the king's retinue of guards and gatekeeper, but Rafe had no illusions about the power distribution in the room. The king alone had as much as his entire retinue combined, and the king was walking toward Kiran. Rafe crossed the room to put himself in front of his retainer, bristling with his stolen power and the desire to fight, kill, and rip apart any threat.

Soren paused, surprise crossing his face, and then smiled. "Don't worry. I'm not interested in him."

The king's movements were easy, casual—the behavior of an individual confident in his power. Rafe was much the same, most of the time, but here and now, his uneasiness made him defensive. Even with the power of two ghouls, he wouldn't match the king's strength. Soren brushed past Rafe as if he were no more interesting than a blade of grass, and bent over Alma's prone form. He brushed a finger down the side of her face, and she stirred to consciousness.

"Don't be afraid," he murmured in Caddenese, his voice soft and comforting, and Alma stared at him with confusion, but not fear. "You're safe here." Soren turned to Rafe and switched languages. "The boy thinks she can create portals; can she?"

"Yes. But I don't think she understands the power."

"Where am I?" Alma's age showed through in her voice, frail and soft. She sat up.

"Safe," Soren reassured her, but her eyes turned to Rafe and Kiran, and then around the room.

"Where have you taken me?"

"Away from that hellish place," Rafe said. "Away from the lunatic Sharim."

He wasn't sure what he'd anticipated—maybe gratitude for saving her life—but she flew into a shrieking rage, throwing insults and threats at him with far more power than he'd expected out of a waifish old lady.

"You would rather I'd left you there to die?" he asked.

"Yes!" she screamed. "The path ends with Shadelin! Where am I now? I have betrayed the gods' plans!"

"But... Hadn't you already, by sending morroul away instead of feeding them?"

She shook her head, glaring. The screaming fit was over. She sagged into the sofa cushions, exhaustion on her old features. "The gods spoke to me... The morroul are animals. We were fools to lure them in and feed them."

Soren glanced up at Rafe, but Rafe's attention had shifted to Beah. This affected him more than it did any of the rin. He still appeared stunned and confused, and it was unclear how much he'd heard or comprehended from Alma's rant.

"If you are afraid of the gods' wrath," Soren said, "I can have my gatekeeper return you to your home...but I've seen what happened there. I fear you do not have a home to return to."

Alma was silent, the confusion and anger morphing into shock. Soren, with all the tenderness of a parent comforting their child, stroked her cheek and smiled.

"I think you should come with me," he said. "I will see you are comfortable until you're ready to make a decision. I think you'll find this world has much to offer."

She nodded, and Soren straightened up and gestured to one of his guards. The rin crossed the room and helped Alma to her feet, murmuring comforting words she probably didn't understand.

Rafe wasn't sure he liked the idea of the king taking Alma away. She was Beah's only connection to his world, his old home, but...from what Rafe knew about Beah, maybe he'd be happy to have a completely fresh start.

"What will you do with her?" Rafe asked.

"Nothing heinous, if you are worried about it."

Soren's eyes raked over Rafe from head to toe, and Rafe had a sudden jolt of fear. This was the longest interaction he'd ever had with the king. He'd had to visit him once, to make a bond of loyalty, but it had been a matter of introductions, a quick reading of words and sharing of blood, and he was on his way.

"You should be more worried about yourself and your lover," Soren murmured, moving closer to Rafe. "You could have killed him."

Chapter Twenty-Seven

RAFE

"I saved him."

Soren scoffed, but stopped only a few steps away. "You are foolish."

Anger burned through Rafe, and he forced himself to remain where he was, to not challenge the king's approach—not to give in to the urges in him, driving him to attack, to defend his home and his family.

"If you don't want to turn your companion into a puddle of inept, mindless goo, I would advise you to stop overwhelming his mind with foolish power trips."

"Foolish—?"

"He feels what you feel, Rafe." Soren closed the distance between them and lay a hand on Rafe's cheek. His palm was not the baby-soft silk of some people in power, but callused from handling weapons. "Human minds are delicate. Such a sudden influx of power is too much for him to handle. I could have you arrested for endangerment."

"I would never," Rafe said, his voice sharp. He was hurting Eamon by having so much power? The revelation was like a bucket of cold water on the fire of his rage. "How do I fix it?"

"Give it to me," Soren said. "I can handle it, and so can my companions. We are old and experienced with such power. You and Eamon are barely more than infants in comparison."

Rafe was young, but an infant? How old was Soren? It was a question for another time though. Eamon was in danger.

He lowered himself to one knee. "Please take it from me. I'd never forgive myself if harm came to Eamon because of my ignorance."

Soren's fingers combed through his hair, nails scraping back along his scalp in a soothing way. "I know," he murmured. "I feel the same way about all my subjects, Rafe. As a good leader should." He lowered himself to his knees in front of Rafe, tilted his head up with a gentle touch to his chin, and kissed him.

At the touch of the strange lips, Rafe went tense. He'd never thought about this side of the feeding. He'd been so rarely fed upon, and was so careful with how he fed on Kiran, he hadn't realized... His chest tightened at the thought of a feeding, a full, intimate, deep feeding like so many others enjoyed... Here, with the king, in front of everyone...

Soren broke the kiss. "Just this," he murmured against Rafe's lips. "This is all I want from you. May I?"

His heart pounding, Rafe nodded, and the next time the king's lips touched his, the strength and the drives to fight and fuck and feed left him. Soren's pale hands tightened on his head, and the king let out a moan as he drew the excess power out of Rafe. It would have been just as easy for Soren to keep going, to draw Rafe's life out as Rafe had done to the ghouls, and the thought made him shudder. It wasn't common practice for rin to feed on each other. It certainly made him appreciate, even more deeply, the trust Eamon and Kiran had shown him.

As the king drew back, he pulled away not only physically, but mentally too. Rafe hadn't been aware the king was in his thoughts again. Another shudder wracked his body. Soren was so strong.

"You've had an interesting adventure, Rafe of Seacliff." Soren's voice was low, his pale face distracted and concerned. It wasn't the kind of expression one liked to see on their king's face.

"I only wanted to get my lover back, Your Majesty," Rafe said, and Soren seemed to realize his face had betrayed his thoughts. He smiled and brought his hand to Rafe's cheek in a comforting gesture.

"You did nothing wrong. In fact, you may have done us a huge favor."

"I did?" Everything was surreal. He was kneeling on the floor in front of the rin who controlled everything from Seacliff to the inner grasslands, dozens of days' travel away. The rin who could do anything he wanted, and no one would protest. Soren was stern and fair by reputation, but not overly kind. Rafe had had something Soren wanted. Maybe he still did.

"The ghouls have been coming through to our world for some time," Soren said. "You know this very well."

"Yes." Rafe cast an anxious glance to his bed where Eamon lay, still asleep. The gods-cursed ghouls had been the bane of his existence for years now.

"You figured out why."

"Alma?"

Soren shook his head. "Her contribution was made through ignorance. There is a more malicious force at work here."

The shady figure giving orders. It had been there in the ghouls' memories when Rafe stole their lives, but he didn't understand.

"There's a rin in their world, sending them through to ours."

"Yes."

"But why? Our two species have never been allies." It was impossible not to ask the questions, now that Rafe was in front of someone who might be able to give answers. If he didn't find out now, he might never understand—and he might never be able to stop the gods-damned things from terrorizing his people.

"They're animals. Animals can be trained."

"But he's training them to attack his own kind."

Soren chuckled. "Not everyone is so pure of heart as you, Rafe." He brushed the backs of his fingers against Rafe's cheek. "There was a time, long ago, when it was common punishment to send criminals to the world of the ghouls."

It took a moment for the implication of the words to sink in. There was a time when leadership thought letting animals hunt and kill and *eat* criminals in a horrid desert world was a just punishment?

And one of them had survived.

"How long ago?" Rafe asked.

"Hundreds of years."

A rin at least as old as Rafe, a dangerous criminal.

This was about revenge.

Soren watched Rafe's face and smiled when he determined Rafe had reached the correct conclusion. Rafe looked up and met the king's eyes, angry and afraid.

"I've suspected for some time, but couldn't be certain," Soren said and stood. "Your adventure has confirmed it. I may even know who we're dealing with now."

Rafe remained on his knees, hands folded in his lap. It wasn't about respect now. He just didn't think he remembered how to move.

"My king... The implications of this..."

Soren paced a few steps away. His shoulders rose and fell in a sigh. "You're no fool."

"Can you stop him?" The words slipped out before Rafe thought them through. He shook his head. "Apologies, Your Majesty. It's not my place."

The king chuckled. He turned back, his boots clicking softly as he crossed the stone floor to the bed where Eamon lay.

Rafe stood. Even without the extra power, he was ready to protect Eamon at all costs.

"You've impressed me, Rafe. The amount of power you held...at your age...and your companion surviving it is a feat too. Your bond is strong." Soren stood by the bed gazing down at Eamon with an oddly affectionate expression on his face. After a moment, he turned to Rafe and fixed him with that same strange affection.

Rafe smiled slightly, but bowed his head. "Thank you for your kind words, Your Majesty."

Soren paced to his small retinue, hands clasped behind him. He cut a beautiful and intimidating figure. And even with all the power he'd just drawn from Rafe, he was poised and reserved, measuring his words without a hint of aggression. "I am not certain what the future holds now, Rafe, but if this conflict cannot be resolved quickly, I may need to call on your strength. If a day comes when I call to you, can I rely on you to be at my side?"

The words stunned Rafe to silence. Of course, the answer he should give, immediate and unflinching, was clear. But he also wasn't one to give a response simply because it was expected of him. Yet, too much had happened that day for him to give the question proper consideration. He had no idea what it meant to be at the king's side during a conflict—a war, if he understood correctly—but he imagined it would be dangerous. But if a vengeful rin was ordering ghouls through to their world, things wouldn't be getting any safer either. He swallowed and nodded. "Of course, Your Majesty."

"Good."

A soft noise from the bed drew his attention. Eamon lifted a hand to his face and groaned.

"The sleeping beauty awakes," Soren said, voice light and amused. "Go to your lover, Rafe."

After the necessary shows of respect had been observed, Soren turned to his gatekeeper. She made a simple arcing gesture with one hand, and a doorway of shimmering light appeared. A much more elegant portal than Rafe's tattered gateways. Once the king was out of sight, along with Alma and his retinue, Rafe virtually threw himself at Eamon, scrambling onto the bed at his lover's side.

"Eamon? Are you all right? How do you feel?"

Eamon blinked a few times and then surged to life, looking around with a gasp. "We're home!"

"We're home," Rafe agreed, a smile breaking across his face.

Eamon's eyes shone with moisture, and tears spilled down his cheeks. He threw his arms around Rafe's shoulders and hugged him, sobbing in relief and joy.

Kiran subtly gestured Beah toward the door, giving Rafe and Eamon the privacy they desperately needed.

When the door had shut with a soft click behind the others, Rafe and Eamon separated and gazed at each other. The relief at seeing his lover back in their bed where he belonged was enough to drive Rafe to tears, but he forced himself to lean on the familiarity of taking care and control first.

"Are you injured anywhere? I can summon Elena."

Eamon shook his head, smiling. "I'm fine."

"Hungry? Thirsty?"

"I'm *fine*," Eamon insisted, his smile widening.

He might be dirty from weeks of rough living, skinnier than he'd been last time they'd been together, but none of it seemed to impact his enthusiasm at being back home in Rafe's arms.

Rafe was also aware his partner had one thing in mind—he had to admit, it was at the forefront of his mind too. Their bond made it hard to misinterpret the other's motives. A little smile tugged at Rafe's lips, and he kept going.

"Are you tired? I can leave you to sleep."

At the teasing undertone of Rafe's words, Eamon chuckled. He leaned forward and spoke in a low voice. "If you try to leave, I will tackle you and drag you back here."

"Oh my, that sounds terrifying," Rafe murmured, but he couldn't keep the smile off his face. Their teasing might have gone on and on, and any another night perhaps it would have, but a surge of longing and relief tightened Rafe's chest, and he put his arms around his lover again. "I missed you, Eamon."

"I missed you too." He planted a kiss on Rafe's throat. Then another.

Rafe sighed and tilted his head back; there would be no stopping now. No more words, no more tears, no more apologies. He turned his head to catch his lover's mouth, and Eamon moaned at the touch of his lips. A desire rose in Rafe, a need as powerful as what he'd felt when he was high on the savage energy of the ghouls.

Eamon felt it, too, and grabbed a fistful of Rafe's cloak to pull him to the center of the bed. There, he pushed Rafe down and straddled his hips. The kisses were sloppy with need and enthusiasm, and Rafe found himself laughing as they both tried to disrobe without separating their mouths. Eamon laughed, too, equal parts joy and relief.

"Brief respite," Rafe suggested against Eamon's lips, "to shed our clothing?"

Eamon groaned and plunged his tongue into Rafe's mouth again, hands clutching his face, and Rafe had to take control and flip their positions, pinning Eamon on his back before the human would let him pull away long enough to strip. While Rafe tossed his clothing haphazardly on a chair near the bed, Eamon squirmed out of his own garb and threw it on the floor. The sight of his lover's naked body gave Rafe pause, as a surge of emotion bubbled up and clutched at his chest. He loved Eamon more than he'd ever known was possible. His absence had hurt like a physical injury, and the sight of him here, after coming so close to losing him, was overwhelming.

Eamon's pale body had changed some in the time he was gone. He was leaner, bones and muscles more visible under his dusty skin than they'd been before he disappeared.

"You're beautiful, you know," Eamon said, and Rafe looked up, realizing he was being scrutinized as well.

"I'm like a simple blade of grass next to your own flowering beauty," he replied, and Eamon scoffed.

"Flatterer. Bring that talented mouth over here." Eamon's hand moved down to wrap around his own cock and stroke it a couple times, bringing a moan to his lips.

Rafe's breath caught in his throat, and he was back on the bed and kissing his lover in an instant. Eamon's hand kept moving on himself until Rafe pushed it away and wrapped his fist around Eamon's cock.

"Gods, you drive me wild, Eamon."

Eamon smiled and wrapped his arms around Rafe, hands coasting up and down his bare back, their mouths and tongues pressed together, breathing each other's breath.

The foreplay only lasted a moment longer before Eamon was spreading his legs wide, rocking his hips up, begging silently. Neither needed to speak a word for the other to know exactly what they wanted. The long, slow lovemaking would have to wait. For now, they both needed relief and reassurance. They were too eager, too desperate for the other's touch.

Rafe broke the kiss long enough to grab a bottle of oil from the bedside drawer. Eamon wrapped his hands behind his knees and pulled his ass up, legs as far apart as possible. It might have been a humiliating position to some, but to Rafe it was one of the most perfect sights his lover could treat him to. He worked quickly to apply the oil. It didn't matter they were both a mess, covered in sweat and dirt from another world. The only thing that mattered to either of them was the other, and the sensations sparking through their bodies and across their bond.

Eamon moaned as Rafe breached his body.

"Gods I missed this," Eamon whispered, even as his brow furrowed at the intrusion. "I need this. I love you."

"I love you too," Rafe returned, and pushed, knowing Eamon's needs, easily interpreting his exact desires through their connection. He needed to be possessed, reassured with vigor and enthusiasm that this was all real, that they would not be parted ever again. Rafe needed it too, and only took a moment to build up to full, hard thrusts which knocked little whimpers and moans of pleasure from Eamon each time their bodies impacted.

Rafe let their bond fall wide open, Eamon's pleasure and his joining simultaneously. He bent over his lover, grateful for the height difference that allowed him to keep up the rhythm while he took Eamon's mouth again. Eamon moaned and let go of one of his legs to grip his own cock again, and Rafe gasped at the jolt of pleasure that shot through his mind at the added touch. He wasn't feeding from Eamon as they made love—his partner was too weak, and Soren had left Rafe well sated—but the sensations and emotions filled another part of him which had been empty, leaving him exhilarated and content.

"Oh gods," Eamon murmured. "I missed this, Rafe. I missed this. I missed you." His hand tightened around his length, stroking hard in time with Rafe's thrusts. Words continued spilling out of his lips between gasps and whimpers. "I love you. I love you. I love—oh gods!"

Eamon's orgasm surged through the bond, and the overwhelming pleasure and joy and relief drove him over the edge. He moaned his own "I love you" as his cock pulsed inside Eamon.

They collapsed in each other's arms, gasping and smiling. Eamon pecked little kisses all over Rafe's sweat-glistened skin.

"Gods, that was good," he whispered, and Rafe smiled again.

"It was perfect."

Chapter Twenty-Eight

BEAH

Beah followed the dark stranger, Kiran, still huddled under Eamon's borrowed cloak. His head was spinning with everything he'd just been through and with the foreign words of passersby he somehow understood.

"Are you hurt?" Kiran asked after a few minutes.

"No," Beah said. It wasn't completely true. His feet hurt from running on stone. His face hurt from the priest's backhand slap. His stomach hurt from hunger. More than anything, though, he wanted something to wrap around his chest, to ease the weight and subdue the movements of his breasts. He'd been hugging himself, trying to comfort himself in this strange place, but it wasn't helping much.

"I need clothes," he said finally. The words came out in Eamon's language, the language the king had put into his head. Had it erased Caddenese? He didn't know how to test it. Did it matter? It was one less thing to remind him of his old home.

"Of course," Kiran said, and took a turn at the next corner to lead Beah down some stairs.

The place they were in was unlike anything he'd ever seen before. At home, buildings were brown clay and red stone, dusty and small. This building was enormous. They walked down long flights of steps and endless gray stone corridors, and passed through doorways with wood panels that closed firmly in place and had to be opened by turning a round handle.

"We're heading for the bathhouse," Kiran said. "I'll have someone there run and fetch clothes for you."

Beah hugged himself tighter. Bathhouse? He didn't want to strip in front of anyone. He'd had enough for one day, being forced to nudity in front of the priest for the cleansing rituals.

"I understand your...predicament," Kiran said softly. "You'll have privacy."

They passed through a doorway into a room, staggering with its foreignness. The air was hot and wet, like the moments after a rare summer rainstorm. And water *everywhere*. Pools of it in the floor. Tubs of it scattered around the room. People bathing in it. He'd never quite gotten over the awe of the river during his travels, and now here he was, nowhere near a river, yet there was so much water.

"Where does it all come from?" he asked.

"What?"

"The water."

Kiran smiled. "Underground." He waved down someone wearing a simple dark blue dress, and she joined them. "Gloria, please find clothes for our guest. Beah, what kind of clothes do you want?"

"Like yours," he said immediately. "Like Eamon's."

Kiran nodded and described briefly what the girl should bring, and even though Beah understood the words, he didn't know what the different items would look like. He was trusting Kiran more than he'd trusted anyone in a long time, but he didn't have much choice. Once the girl, Gloria, had departed, Kiran took a seat on a nearby bench and peeled himself out of his boots and socks.

"Is any of this familiar to you?" Kiran asked. "You look like an owl with eyes so large."

"No."

Smiling a gentle smile, Kiran explained everything and offered to have a servant help, but Beah shook his head sharply. Even that was met with gentleness, and Kiran merely had a servant set up a folding wall around one of the tubs for privacy, and then everyone left Beah alone.

Everything here was strange, but so far, everyone seemed kind. The idea of servants was astonishing to him—especially the notion of servants waiting on *him*. If anything, he expected to *be* a servant. And maybe he would be. Maybe after he was cleaned up and dressed, he would be taken to some servant quarters and trained to go fetch clothes for people or help scrub someone's back.

It didn't matter. He sank into the warm water up to his neck and let himself enjoy the moment for what it was.

Afterward, dressed in clothes much like what he'd admired on Eamon—compressing, high-collared, and thick enough to disguise the form of his body—he followed Kiran to another large room, this one full of tables. They sat together while Beah ate his fill of strange, delicious foods.

A tall, pale-haired woman approached and threw her arms around Kiran, and began bombarding him with questions. When did they return? Where was Rafe? Was Eamon back too? Beah listened to them curiously. The woman named Orienna was fascinated most of all by Kiran's recollection of the king's conversation with Rafe, and the king's mention of calling Rafe to his side.

"Did Rafe agree?"

"When the king says he wants you at his side, you don't turn him down."

She frowned and glanced away. "War, huh?"

Kiran shrugged. "I don't pretend to have the mind of a strategist, but maybe if we make a decisive strike when the enemy's not expecting it, we won't come to war."

"I don't like it."

"Me neither," Kiran agreed, "but I don't like sitting here while the ghouls pick us off either."

The conversation tapered off there, and Orienna departed with niceties aimed at them both. As the pain in Beah's stomach stopped distracting him, he paid more attention to the surroundings. The huge room had windows, but no air seemed to flow through them. He stuffed one last bite of food into his mouth and got up. There were other people in the room, but Kiran had intentionally seated them far away from everyone else, so he didn't feel too awkward getting up and walking to the nearest window. He was a stranger here, but it comforted and fascinated him that everyone looked different. He didn't stand out the way Eamon had in Beah's home village.

A clear covering over the window allowed him to see to the outside without being affected by the elements. Beyond it, grass, thick and dark green stretched out for some distance before it met the gray-blue sky and stopped. Someone stepped up beside him and he turned to find Kiran had joined him.

"Different from what you're used to, isn't it?"

Beah smiled. "Yes. Eamon said he lived near the sea. Where is it?"

"It's out there," Kiran said. "Below us. Want to go see?"

Beah nodded and followed his new friend through a few more corridors until they were outside. Immediately, Beah shivered and pulled his borrowed cloak around himself again. It was cool as a desert evening, and around them, everything was rich and dark. The sky was cloudless, but not as bright and clear as back home. The sun shone low in the sky but didn't burn through Beah's clothes and skin like he was accustomed to. The grass was a darker shade of green than anything he'd seen before, and he wondered if it was always like this. The stone path they followed out of the manor was lined on either side with plants, multi-colored foliage with uniquely shaped leaves, and occasionally a stalk of purple or white flowers.

Once they were a short distance from the building, the wind picked up. It rustled through the tall grass and whipped Beah's cloak around his feet. He'd thought the forest between his home and the mountains was as different as things could get from what he was used to, but he was wrong.

"Is it always like this?" he asked, raising his voice.

"Windy?" Kiran asked. "Yes. The sea creates the winds."

"And dark? And cold?"

"Around here, yes," Kiran said and chuckled. "We're far north."

They left the stone walkway and began plowing through tall grass. Beah followed in Kiran's footsteps until the dark-skinned rin stopped and gestured for him to stand at his side.

They stood close to the edge of a cliff, and Beah moved forward until he was able to see over the edge. Water crashed into the stones below, steel-gray shattering into explosions of white foam over and over again with a soothing rhythm. He watched for several minutes, fascinated by the motion on the shore. The sea itself seemed to hold still the farther out he looked, with only occasional small white splashes to indicate it wasn't solid ground. It went on forever and ever until it joined with the dark blue horizon.

"It's amazing," Beah said. Eamon had said it was like a desert made of water, but such a description didn't do it justice. The desert was motionless, oppressive, stoic. The sea was alive with power and fury and beauty.

When he turned to Kiran, he found the rin smiling at him again. Beah's gaze slid past Kiran to the building some distance away—the building he'd been in moments ago. It was just as massive as he'd suspected. He counted three windows tall and ten across, all of it made of pale gray stone, except the roof, which was darker and slanted. The structure was absolutely foreign. Everything here was foreign...but maybe that wasn't a bad thing. Beyond the building, the ground sloped down, a forest stretching out on the other side. It seemed as endless as the sea.

"Ready to head back?" Kiran asked.

Beah nodded and found a smile curving his lips. It might take some time to get used to it, but things were better here. They had to be.

Chapter Twenty-Nine

EAMON

As much as he would have liked to do nothing but make love for days, concern drove Eamon to get up and dress the next morning. They'd bathed, he'd eaten, and they'd made love again before falling asleep in each other's arms. And, all right, they'd made love again after waking up, but after, Eamon insisted on getting out of bed.

"I want to check on Beah."

"He's been with Kiran. He's fine." But Rafe got up, too, pulling on clothes. Now that they were home, they would have to return to business as usual eventually. No point in putting it off for days.

"Speaking of Kiran, he's outside the door."

A knock punctuated Rafe's words, and Eamon smiled before calling out, "Come in!"

They were both dressed, but Kiran came in with one hand over his eyes and a grin on his face. "Are you decent? Am I interrupting?"

"If you were interrupting, we wouldn't have let you in," Rafe said.

Kiran chuckled and dropped his hand to his side. "There's someone here to see you, Eamon."

"Here? Like—"

Before Eamon finished the thought, Kiran pushed the door open farther, and three people came spilling into the room chattering excitedly. Eamon barely had time to recognize Rose, Lionel, and Tuomas before they were burying him in hugs and kisses and praise and scoldings and so much emotion Eamon couldn't respond to it all. He laughed and hugged them, not even trying to answer their five thousand overlapping questions.

They backed off in an instant when Rafe cleared his throat, scrambling into a line side by side to face him and bow, but he didn't scold them for bursting into his personal chambers. Instead, he crossed the room to where they stood and sighed.

"I feel I may owe you three an apology," he said. "When Eamon disappeared, I was harsh with you out of my own fear and frustration. I know you were just as anxious as I was. It was unfair."

"You were completely justified, my lord," Lionel said. "We should have protected him better."

"No. You're human. Four humans should never face a ghoul alone. I should have—"

"All right," Kiran cut in. "Enough guilt. Everyone's alive. There's no more to be done."

Relieved smiles flickered across every face in the room. Eamon looked past his friends to Kiran. "Where's Beah?"

"Still asleep. Yesterday was rather overwhelming."

He could imagine. After all, it wasn't too long ago when he'd been thrown into a foreign world with no time to prepare and no idea what to expect.

"Eamon, before you run off with your friends," Rafe said, "I'd like to talk to you and Kiran."

Eamon and Kiran exchanged a glance. The other three humans recognized a dismissal when they heard one.

"Eamon," Tuomas said. "Lunch in the main hall later, okay? We want to hear everything. We'll track you down and drag you away if we must."

"No need." Eamon laughed. "I'll be there."

After more hugs and kisses, his friends made their departures, and the room fell silent around the three of them. Eamon and Rafe had closed their bond down to its normal, safe level after the wide-open sharing during their reunion last night, so Eamon wasn't able to pick up on exactly what was on Rafe's mind, except for the tension there.

Kiran glanced between the two of them, brows drawn. "What's wrong?"

"Nothing's wrong." Rafe gestured to the sofa, and while Kiran and Eamon settled onto it, he seated himself in the adjacent chair. "I want to address something with you both." He pressed his lips together, and Eamon's anxiety began to increase. What possibly needed to be addressed in such a way? What was making Rafe nervous?

"Eamon, you are aware that while you were gone I fed on Kiran?"

"Yes," Eamon said slowly, glancing over at Kiran. "I watched you feed on him after you got injured by those guards."

"Right," Rafe said. "I want to make sure there are no hard feelings between you two."

Eamon and Kiran exchanged a glance again, and Eamon laughed in relief. "You want to make sure I'm not jealous?"

"Either of you," Rafe said. "I know how feeding can easily lead to thoughts of romance and intimacy... It *is* intimate. But... Kiran, you understand—"

Kiran smiled. "That you're not in love with me or attracted to me? Yes, I understand, my lord. I didn't let you feed from me in hopes you'd fall in love with me. I did it because I didn't want to watch you starve to death."

"And I'm not jealous or upset you fed on someone else while I was gone," Eamon added. "You have to feed. I'm not a fool. If anything, I'm grateful to Kiran for offering himself."

Rafe looked back and forth between the two of them, blinking. "So no animosity between you two?"

"No animosity here," Eamon said.

"Here either," Kiran said. "I love you both. I'm happy to serve in any way I can. I never expected more."

Eamon twisted in his seat and threw his arms around Kiran. "Thank you for not letting him starve to death."

Kiran laughed and returned the embrace, and Rafe piled onto the sofa with them in a rare show of affection, his arms around them both. Once they'd satisfied their need for hugs, Eamon brought up the other concern on his mind.

"So...what happens if the king does call you to his side?"

Rafe shrugged and returned to his chair, putting some distance between them to help regain his lord mindset. "I guess I go."

"What about me?"

"You'll come with me."

"And Beah?"

"It depends on what he wants," Rafe said. "We'll find him a role he enjoys."

"And me?" Kiran asked, hesitant.

"You're in line to take over Seacliff Manor, if you wish it."

"I don't," he said immediately. "I want to come with you. Give Orienna the manor. She's better suited for leadership than I am."

Rafe smiled gently and nodded. "Duly noted, Kiran."

"I don't want to go to war," Eamon whispered. "I don't want either of you to go either."

Rafe slid out of his chair to kneel on the floor at Eamon's feet and took his hands. "I don't want to go to war either, Eamon. Trust me. I don't want to put either of you in danger by taking you with me, but something big is happening around us, and if the king thinks I can help...I have to try. I have to do as he asks."

Eamon swallowed a lump in his throat. "I hope he doesn't ask."

"Let's not worry about it for now," Rafe said. He pulled Eamon's hands forward and kissed his knuckles. "You're safe. You're home. We're together."

"We should celebrate," Kiran said. "We should have a welcome home ball."

"I don't need a ball," Eamon protested.

"Then let's have a ball for Beah, to introduce him to everyone."

"Gods, you're persistent." Eamon rolled his eyes, but Rafe was smiling—the decision had been made. Kiran loved to dress nicely and dance with as many people as possible. Rafe loved to see Eamon dress nicely, and he loved to dance with Eamon in front of everyone, reminding the entire manor of his love and dedication. Eamon wondered how Beah would react to dressing nicely and dancing.

Kiran sprang up off the sofa, a huge grin brightening his face. "I'll go get arrangements started."

"Please do," Rafe said, and a moment later, the door closed behind Kiran and they were alone. Rafe got up and pressed Eamon down on the sofa, pinning him under enthusiastic kisses. "I think we have some time before you need to meet your friends for lunch."

Eamon laughed. "You're incorrigible," he said, but he couldn't find it in himself to mind. Maybe the king would summon Rafe to his side tomorrow, or in six months, but for now they were together. He forced the worries to the back of his mind and focused on the body against his, firm and strong and protective.

"I love you," Rafe whispered in his ear. "Every time I touch you, every time I look at you, every time I hear your voice, I fall in love with you again. Words don't exist to express how I feel."

"Then show me," Eamon replied, and his mind flooded with such warmth and affection it brought tears to his eyes.

He pulled Rafe into a kiss, and for the first time in weeks, the fear that had been plaguing him was completely gone. Everything was all right now. He was home. He was safe.

Acknowledgements

Huge thank you to Amanda and Deanna for their boundless encouragement and enthusiasm, and to my husband for his patience, love, support, and terrible jokes.

About the Author

Leigh M. Lorien is a queer author who got her start at the tender age of five, writing and illustrating her own Sonic the Hedgehog stories. Fortunately, her writing has improved in the subsequent decades. Nowadays, Leigh's stories primarily lean toward science fiction, fantasy, and urban fantasy, but she has had some contemporary pieces sneak out of her head. Regardless of genre, her books will usually include sarcasm, strong relationships (romantic and platonic), polyamory/non-monogamy, magic, music, animals, mental illness, and less-frequently-represented queer identities.

When she's not writing, Leigh enjoys gardening, photography, travel, music, Renaissance festivals, doing hair-color experiments in her bathroom, and going on any kind of adventure involving the outdoors (unless it's cold, screw that). If you want to know her better or see pictures of her many fur-children, she's most active on Twitter and Instagram.

Pronouns: She/her, they/them

Email: leighmwrites@gmail.com

Facebook: www.facebook.com/leighmwrites

Twitter: @leighmlorien

Website: www.leighmlorien.wordpress.com

Also Available from NineStar Press

Connect with NineStar Press

www.ninestarpress.com

www.facebook.com/ninestarpress

www.facebook.com/groups/NineStarNiche

www.twitter.com/ninestarpress

www.tumblr.com/blog/ninestarpress

9 781951 057022